MW01038608

BEAN STALKER

AND OTHER HILARIOUS SCARYTALES

BEANS

KIERSTEN WHITE

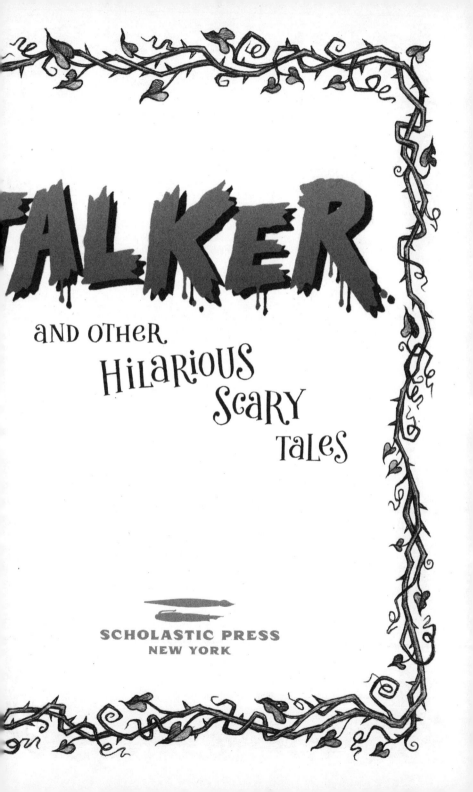

...TALKER

AND OTHER Hilarious Scary Tales

SCHOLASTIC PRESS
NEW YORK

For Elena, Jonah, and Ezra
My little Fridays in human form

Text copyright © 2017 by Kiersten Brazier
Illustrations copyright © 2017 by Karl Kwasny

Library of Congress Cataloging-in-Publication Data

Names: White, Kiersten, author. | Title: Beanstalker and other hilarious scarytales / Kiersten White. | Description: First edition. | New York, NY : Scholastic Press, 2017. | Summary: Snow White is a vampire, Little Red Riding Hood is a zombie, and Cinderella is an arsonist–and that is only some of the mayhem the reader will find in this collection of fractured fairy tales. | Identifiers: LCCN 2016040578 (print) | LCCN 2016044412 (ebook) | ISBN 9780545940603 (hardcover) | ISBN 9780545945868 | Subjects: LCSH: Fairy tales. | Horror tales. | Humorous stories. | CYAC: Characters in literature–Fiction. | Fairy tales. | Horror stories. | Humorous stories. | LCGFT: Horror fiction. | Humorous fiction | Classification: LCC PZ8.W5795 Be 2017 (print) | LCC PZ8.W5795 (ebook) | DDC 813.6 [Fic]–dc23 | LC record available at https://lccn.loc.gov/2016040578.

10 9 8 7 6 5 4 3 2   17 18 19 20 21

Printed in the U.S.A.   23   First edition, August 2017

Book design by Carol Ly and Baily Crawford

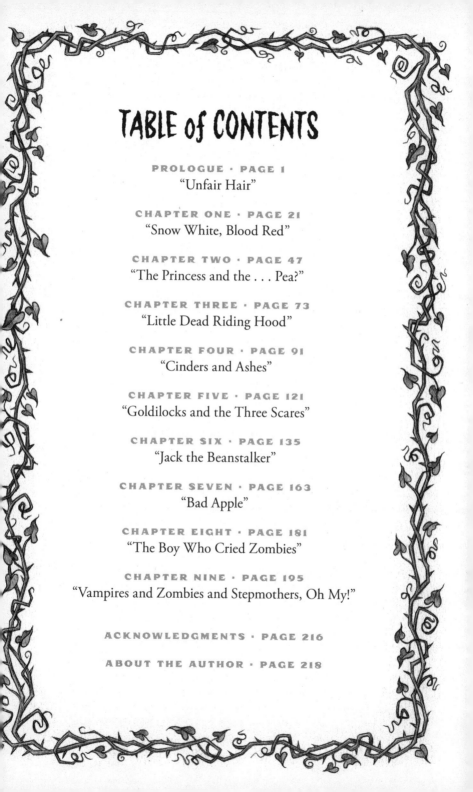

TABLE of CONTENTS

"Unfair Hair"

The horse has asked to let the record show: She didn't *mean* to kill the prince.

But the prince didn't understand the difference between *reign* and *rein*. A king *reigns*, meaning he is in charge of his kingdom. A horse has *reins*, straps that are used to direct it. But the prince assumed that because he would *reign*, he also had free *rein* with the *reins*. Fortunately, the prince at least understood the difference between *rein*, *reign*, and *rain*, otherwise he might have thought he could command the weather, too.

The horse neighed in an annoyed tone, nudging the dead prince with her long nose. She had only aimed for that low-hanging branch to try to knock some sense into him. Instead, she had knocked him clean off and clean out.

But look! His chest moved up and down. He was still breathing. Shaking her mane in relief, and refusing to stick around while we talked about the difference between *mane*, *main*, and *Maine*, the horse trotted away.

The prince lay in the middle of a vast forest. On one side was a castle with a very tall tower. There was a lot of activity at that castle—soldiers running here and there, calling out a name, searching for someone. A soldier shouted that a horse was missing from the stables, too.

Hmmm.

On the other side of the forest was a castle where no one moved at all during the day. It was as though the entire castle wanted to avoid the harsh light of the sun and only came out after sunset, like creatures of the night.

Hmmmmm.

In between the two castles were a few small villages. There was the occasional cottage in the woods just awaiting a granddaughter, or a clever tailor, or a boy made out of baked goods.

There were also wolves and bears going about,

minding their own business, unaware that very soon they would be descended upon by monsters. Or little girls. In this book, they might be the same thing.

With a groan, the prince sat up. He rubbed his head. If he knew the difference, he'd know that he now had neither *rein* nor *reign*. He was alone, in the middle of a forest. And piercing the sky, just a few yards from where he sat, was a lone tower.

The prince hated towers.

They were ugly. They made your legs burn and your breath catch in your chest if you had to huff all the way to the top of them. They were very difficult to keep clean, what with all the stones and dusty stairs and little animals taking up residence in them. And, until very recently, he had been held prisoner in one.

That last reason is probably a better reason than the others to hate towers.

His first impulse was to burn the tower down. (There are much more reasonable ways of dealing with towers! First, find out what the zoning ordinances are for the kingdom. Are towers allowed? What are the height restrictions? What is the tower being used for? Is it a commercial tower in a residential district? Or a residential tower in an area zoned for retail? Are all of its licenses current and valid? After doing the research, write a letter to the local kingdom council insisting they open up an inquiry to look into whether or not the tower is legal. After waiting several months with no reply, write another letter. This time, say you will be consulting a lawyer. Then you'll need to find a lawyer who specializes in tower law, and . . . You know what, on second thought, the prince is probably onto something with his burning idea.)

But before he could even gather up enough tinder for a campfire, much less a towerfire, he heard the most *beautiful* voice. The prince hurried to the edge of the trees.

The ground around the tower was cleared in a circle. The tower loomed high in the sky, three or four stories tall, unlike this book, which is ten stories tall. Rough gray stones ascended to the sky. There was no door, not even a window until the

top of the tower. That window was open, and from it the voice rang out like a doorbell. Some people have voices like church bells, but this one was less regal and more "come on answer the door come on *come on.*"

The prince understood her urgency. He himself had called out countless times from his tower, and no one ever answered anymore. Well, today, *he* would be *her* answer. He was about to shout up to her when another figure came out of the forest only a few steps away from him. The woman didn't notice him. She wore a long black dress, and her dark hair was pinned into a no-nonsense bun. Her skin was paler than chalk, and she carried a burlap sack filled with something . . . wriggling.

"A witch!" the prince hissed.

"Rapunzel!" the witch cried. "Rapunzel!" She waited a few moments, then shouted in a much witchier tone, "RAPUNZEL!"

"What?" came the sweet reply. The prince squinted, longing to catch a glimpse of Rapunzel, but she remained hidden.

"Rapunzel," the witch shouted, "let down your fair hair!"

From the window slid a length of hair, golden and shining in the sun. The prince was too far away to see clearly, but it was thicker than his arm, as thick as his thigh, even. What glorious hair! The hair reached all the way from the window to the ground.

The witch, still holding the squirming bag, walked forward through the clearing. The prince shifted, and a traitorous twig snapped! Once he was king, he would have that twig found and burned at the stake.

He managed to retreat behind a tree just before the witch turned and caught sight of him. But it was too late for the witch. That poor maiden, trapped in a tower with no door! The prince had figured it all out. The witch must climb the hair-rope up and down. Though what dark purpose the squirming bag held, the prince could only imagine. (He chose not to imagine it. Witches are very scary! I don't blame the prince for deciding not to think too much about it. Though if he were truly princely, he would have charged out of the forest and demanded she release her prey. Let's not be too hard on him, though. He's just been knocked unconscious by a grouchy horse, and apparently has been locked up in a tower for a very long time. Maybe he'll get princelier as the book goes on.)

The prince retreated farther into the woods to wait. After a few minutes, he heard the witch stomping by. She was muttering to herself.

". . . late for my own wedding now, thanks to the creepy little monster. That tower isn't high enough for something so vile."

The prince gasped. He knew that *vile* was like *evil* spelled another way. He couldn't believe the witch would talk that way about the maiden in the tower! It wasn't fair! Though doubtless the maiden was fair! But the pretty kind of *fair*, not the equality kind of *fair*, nor the pale kind of *fair* (like the witch), nor the cotton-candy-and-bad-rides kind of *fair*!

Goodness, I'm the narrator and even I'm getting confused. Let's move on.

The prince, heeding my suggestion, tiptoed out of the cover of the trees. There was no sign of the witch. There was also no way up the tower now that the maiden's fair hair was gone. The prince considered his options. He could call out to her, but what if a stranger's voice frightened her? She had no doubt been trapped in that tower a long time. He decided on a much sneakier plan.

He cleared his throat. "Rapunzel!" he croaked in his best witch voice. "Rapunzel?"

"What?" came the annoyed reply.

"Let down your fair hair!"

"But we just did that!"

The prince cleared his throat again. "Let down your fair hair!"

"Oh, fine!"

The prince looked nervously over his shoulder. If the witch came back now, he was toast. Figuratively. Or maybe even literally, if she was the turn-unfortunate-princes-into-toast kind of witch. He had never heard of that kind, but you never knew with witches.

The hair slid to a halt in front of him and he grabbed hold of it, still looking back toward the woods.

"Yuck," he said, frowning. Whatever product Rapunzel used in her hair, it was . . . not working. The hair was slippery, almost slimy. So smooth he had a hard time holding tight. And the section beneath his hands had a huge, misshapen lump.

Well! He couldn't judge her. After all, she'd been imprisoned in a tower. She probably just needed a good shampoo or two. Or fifty. He began climbing up the hair, one slippery, icky, slicky handhold at a time. The hair shifted and wriggled under his fingers. He climbed faster, looking straight up at the window.

Finally, gasping for breath, he heaved himself over the sill and tumbled into the room. It was dark after the brilliant sunshine outside. He couldn't see much as his eyes adjusted to the dimness. He wiped his hands on his trousers, hoping the hair-feeling would go away soon. Touching his lucky matches for courage, he threw back his shoulders and stood with his feet apart and his fists on his hips.

"I'm here to—"

"Augh!" Rapunzel screamed.

The prince held up his hands, smiling his most princely smile. But he had been locked away for a long time, so it looked less princely and more a-strange-man-just-climbed-in-your-window-and-you-should-probably-find-a-weapon-ly. "Never fear! I'm here to save you! Quick, before the witch comes back."

"What witch?"

"You know. Black dress. Fair complexion. Mean."

"That's my *stepmother*, you jerk. She's not a witch!"

The prince frowned. "Oh. Well. But she has you trapped in this tower!"

"I'm not trapped."

Maybe she was under a spell. So, not a toast-turning witch. A spell-casting witch. Even worse. Unless you really hate crumbs on your fingers, in which case the first kind would be worse. "Yes, you *are* trapped!

The only way up or down is by climbing your hair, and you can't very well climb your own hair, now, can you?"

Rapunzel spoke very slowly, like the prince was a small child. *"There is a door."*

The prince laughed. She was definitely under a spell! Oh, what stories they would tell their friends after he finished rescuing her and they ran away together! "There's no door! There's only that window."

Rapunzel pointed to the other side of the round room. The prince's eyes were finally adjusting to the dim light inside. He saw that a set of stairs led down.

"But what good are stairs if there is no door?" he asked.

Rapunzel threw her hands up in the air, huffing in exasperation. (*Exasperation* is what you feel when you go to get your favorite cereal out of the pantry and someone put the box back inside *already empty*. Well, maybe you feel rage then. I certainly do.) "Did you bother walking around to the *other side of the tower*?"

"Of course I—" The prince stopped, frowning. He hadn't, had he? (No, he didn't. You would remember, because you just read that part.) "I assumed because of your hair, that—" He stopped again, frowning even frowninglier. Because now that his eyes had adjusted, he saw that Rapunzel did not quite match what he had imagined.

She was tall and round, much like the tower she lived in. Only she was not made of rocks. Few people are.

She was wearing lots of black eyeliner—which accented the killer glare she was giving the prince. Her clothes were black, her fingernails were black, her combat boots were black, and her Mohawk was black, too.

Her *Mohawk*. Which was definitely not a fair length of hair stretching all the way to the ground. "Where is your fair hair?" the prince whispered. A prickle of goose bumps rose on the back of his neck.

"Right here." Rapunzel pointed toward the window. She started hauling up coil after coil after coil. The coils moved on their own as she piled them gently on the floor, stopping a couple times to pat them. "You poor dear," she cooed. "Did the mean man climb up you?"

"That's not hair." The prince backed slowly away.

"Yes, it is! This is my fair hair."

"That is *not* hair!"

"It is!"

"It isn't!"

"It is!"

Oh dear. This could go on for quite some time. Clearly someone is confused. I'm going to request a spell-check to make sure I have the right words.

"This. Is. My. Fair. *Herr!*" Rapunzel shouted, stomping one boot-shod foot.

Ah ha! I see my error now. I thought she was saying *hair*, as in the thing that grows out of your head and on your arms and sometimes on your face far too early, as we will learn about much later. But really she was saying *herr*, which is the German word for "lord"!

"This is my fair Herr!" she said, almost at the end of the length of whatever was coming up through the window. "I won him at the fair, and he's as lordly as any creature there ever was!"

The prince felt behind himself with trembling hands, trying to find the top of the stairs but too scared to turn his back on Rapunzel and her pet. By now, the undulating, wriggling coils filled most of the floor. He really should have asked me to clarify which type of fair Rapunzel had been referring to! And asked for spelling. Spelling things wrong can be very dangerous. (That's why you have so many spelling tests in school. It's not to be exasperating; it's to potentially save your life in a situation exactly like this.)

The prince swallowed nervously. "Why do you live in this tower?"

"Because my stepmother wasn't going to let me keep him anywhere else!"

"Why not?"

Finally, she finished pulling. Over the sill came the largest, hissingest, angriest head of a snake the prince had ever had the misfortune to see.

"Well, because my fair Herr has a terrible appetite. And look! You upset him so much, you made him throw up his supper. Poor Herr!"

The prince remembered the wriggling sack. He remembered the witch—the stepmother—muttering about a vile creature. And he remembered the odd lump he'd climbed past on his way up. He didn't want to imagine what was now in a partially digested pile at the bottom of the tower.

(Don't worry! Because the small pig had been so recently ingested, he survived. He was, at this very moment, running home to his dirt burrow. He couldn't wait to wash snake spit off the hairs of his chinny chin

chin, then tell his two brothers they really needed to invest in better building materials for houses: straw. Sticks. Maybe even bricks! Anything to keep them out of the bellies of other animals.)

Rapunzel, unaware of the fate of the little pig's chinny chin chin, glared at the prince. She stroked her fair Herr on his head. His yellow eyes stared unblinkingly at the prince as his long, forked tongue tickled the air.

Did you know snakes smell with their tongues? I wonder what he thinks the prince smells like!

"Sssssssssssupper," the snake answered.

Oh. Oh! Well. That's unfortunate.

"My stepmother won't be back for a few days. And my fair Herr has to eat. He's not picky. He'll eat anything." Rapunzel raised an eyebrow at the prince. The snake had no eyebrows, but if he did, they would have been raised as well.

The prince's eyebrows would have been raised in terror, but they were oddly missing. Like they had been burned off or something. But his forehead was definitely terrified.

The fair Herr slithered closer.

So the prince, who knew a thing or two about towers and gravity, did the only thing he could think of. He threw

15

himself down the stairs. Falling was faster than walking. Each stone step jarred and bruised him, and he hit

every

      single

          step,

              from the

                  top all the

                      way down to

                          the bottom.

He landed in an unprincely lump on the tile floor. There, he found a cheery kitchen, a series of framed photos of Rapunzel and her fair Herr, and the door he hadn't been bright enough to find.

Limping, he threw open the door and stumbled into the sunshine. As soon as he made it to the trees, a trio of soldiers on horses surrounded him. The one who always delivered his food, Willhelm, gently nudged him.

"It's not fair!" the prince shouted, pointing toward the tower.

"Fair or not, you're coming with us."

"No!" the prince said. "The Herr! The Herr!"

"We'll be careful with your hair," Willhelm said, rolling his eyes at the others. One of the soldiers grabbed the prince and threw him onto his horse. (Feeling guilty for whacking him so thoroughly on the head, she had gone for help. Which was good, because we would have hated for her to be around when Rapunzel was looking for new food for her fair Herr.)

"Back to your own tower, Prince Charring," Willhelm said.

The prince nodded, still dazed from his fall. Back to his own, safe, snakeless tower. "No Herr," he whispered. "It's not fair. *It's not fair.*"

Rapunzel leaned out her window, sighing. She looked at her fair Herr. He was her responsibility. And her stepmother was always nagging about responsibility. They were forbidden to leave the tower, but her poor snakey-poo had to eat!

And eat.

And eat.

And eat . . .

Let's use one word here that has a single meaning we can all agree on: RUN!

Meanwhile, in the Kingdom . . .

One, two, buckle your shoe
Three, four, lock the door
Five, six, sharpen sticks
Seven, eight, bar the gate
Nine, ten, something's hungry again . . .

CHAPTER ONE

"Snow White, Blood Red"

Once upon a time in the next kingdom, several years before the prince learned the difference between fair hair and fair Herr, there lived a queen. There also lived a king, otherwise it would have been a queendom. But he isn't important yet.

This queen wanted, more than anything, to have a baby. (Obviously she had not spent much time around babies. Anyone who has could tell you they're pretty awful. They smell bad, they throw up a lot, and they cry instead of sleeping. But maybe she didn't know this, or maybe she knew and just didn't care.)

Every evening, she sat at her window and watched the bats fly across the pale twilight sky. Which was a weird hobby, but, being queen, she could do whatever she wanted.

This particular evening, a bat flapped to a frantic halt on her windowsill. Its tiny, furry ribs shuddered with breath. Although it was basically a fuzzy black rat with wings, the queen thought it was adorable. Cooing, she reached out to pet it.

It bit down with surprisingly sharp fangs on her finger.

"Ouch!" the queen shouted, scaring the bat away. She shook her hand, and two drops of ruby blood fell to the snowy-white lace of her skirt. "Oh, how beautiful," she crooned with a dreamy sigh. This might be why the king isn't in the story yet. The queen is pretty creepy. He probably spent most of his time hunting or riding or hiding in another part of the castle to avoid her.

"If only I could have a baby with skin as white as snow, hair as black as a bat, and lips as red as blood."

Clasping her hands to her heart, she closed her eyes and wished with all her might that her dream would come true. And, deep within her, something fluttered like the tiny pulse of velvet bat wings.

All through the pregnancy, the queen had gotten thinner, paler, and sicker. She was too weak to leave her room. She only had enough energy to sew. One day, a servant caught her licking the blood away after she accidentally pricked her finger.

"For the baby," she said with a dreamy sigh.

This is getting scary. Let's skip ahead.

The baby was born, covered in blood. Babies are gross. You *were* warned.

She had pale, cold skin, fuzzy black hair, and perfect crimson lips. And instead of a gummy baby mouth, she had several tiny pearls of teeth. *Sharp* teeth.

"Snow White," the queen named her. The midwife didn't mind all the blood, because of Snow White's hypnotic eyes. The servants didn't mind cutting red meat into tiny, baby-size pieces, because she was so beautiful. The queen didn't even mind that Snow White bit her with those sharp, pearly teeth when she wanted to eat. The queen was deliriously happy.

The king was happy, too, that his wife finally had what she wanted and would maybe be less creepy now.

And then the queen died.

That was not happy.

But no one was sad for very long. Snow White was too beautiful for anyone to stay sad. At first, her stained lips and her pure black eyes were uncomfortable to look at. But the longer anyone looked into those bottomless eyes, the more they realized how much they *loved* Snow White. The poor baby!

Snow White was beautiful.

Snow White was good.

Snow White was sweet.

They would do anything Snow White asked.

And they would feed her whatever she wanted.

Yes. Look into those pure black eyes. We love Snow White.

We love Snow White.

The king's new wife stepped out of her carriage. She was late. It didn't seem to matter. It was dusk, which was when everyone in the castle started coming out and getting their work done. Everyone slept all day and stayed up all night, because that was what the king wanted, because that was what Snow White wanted.

The king's new wife watched as they scurried

about—pale, weak, with dark circles under their eyes and vacant expressions.

"Oh dear," she said.

The king had sent her a letter with shaky handwriting. He said that Snow White needed a mother, that Snow White was a dear little thing desperately in need of new company, that Snow White would change the king's new wife's life forever. The king's new wife had thought it odd that he never said anything about how much he wanted her as a wife, or what a good queen she would make. The letter had been entirely about Snow White.

Still. She never turned down a stepchild.

"Isn't it weird how no one here has a tan?" her stepson, Jack, asked, but she shook her head and drew herself up to her tallest, most queenly height.

"Come along, Jack," she said as she swept through the courtyard and into the castle.

The wedding was scheduled for midnight. The king's new wife put on her finest gown, changed her black hair from a no-nonsense bun into cascading curls, and fastened a heavy gold necklace around her throat. She didn't look at all witchlike, despite what certain princes would think upon seeing her at a tower.

"Looking good, Mom!" Jack said.

"Hmm," the king's new wife said, gazing critically at herself in the mirror. Her skin was as fair as new milk. This *fair* is a nice way of saying that she was incredibly pale, prone to horrible sunburns, and didn't look good in very many colors. She was, in fact, as fair as a person could be while still being a person.

That will be important later on.

She made her way regally to the castle chapel. This was her first marriage to a king, and she was excited in spite of herself. But when she got to the chapel, no one was there. A servant meekly informed her that the wedding would take

place in the castle cemetery. By Snow White's request, of course.

The king waited for her there. He was thin and stooped, and his clothes hung on him like a very wealthy scarecrow. He, too, had dark circles under his eyes and a vacant expression on his terribly pale face. But the king's new wife was fairer still.

At his side was a small girl of seven or eight. When she saw the king's new wife, her black eyes lit up with anticipation. Her gaze lingered on the gold at the king's new wife's neck. Snow White licked her beautiful red lips and smiled with her sharp teeth.

The king's new wife smiled back and said her marriage vows to the king.

But when she said, "I do," she was looking at Snow White and thinking, *Oh dear.*

The king died a week later. The king's new wife was now the queen: sole ruler of the kingdom and sole parent to Snow White.

The midnight funeral was an odd affair. No one cried, and the queen insisted on burying him with wreaths of garlic. "It's a custom where I'm from," she said. It wasn't.

The next morning, the queen went into Snow White's room bright and early. The windows were covered with curtains so thick not a whisper of light came through. Snow White lay still and silent as death on her bed. Her hands were clasped on her chest, her face serene and beautiful.

Well, she didn't lie *on* her bed, so much as over it. She hung from a bar, upside down, black hair pooling around her.

The queen ripped down the curtains.

Snow White fell onto the bed, hissing as she covered her eyes.

"Things are going to change around here," the queen said. She touched her golden necklace and smiled pleasantly. "First things first, we are awake during the day and asleep at night."

"But I hate the light. Make it go away!" Snow White wailed and bared her teeth.

The queen folded her arms and raised a single eyebrow. She did not look directly at Snow White.

"Please," Snow White said, her ruby lips trembling tragically. "It hurts my eyes. You don't want to hurt me, do you?"

"I want to do what is best for everyone," the queen said.

"But I feel so weak during the day."

This time, the queen's smile was not so pleasant. "I know, child. I know."

After that, everything was different around the castle. The servants loved the beautiful child with a fierce devotion. They tried to sneak around the queen's horrible, strict rules. So the queen fired them.

She set Snow White to work in their place, scrubbing floors, cleaning rooms, and, though Snow White cried lovely crystal tears, tending the garden. The queen's stepson, Jack, didn't have to do anything. He wasn't even allowed to play with Snow White so she would have a friend.

The new queen was evil, the people of the kingdom whispered. She had killed the king and kept Snow White imprisoned in the castle. After a while of the queen's rule, all that remained were the rumors of Snow White's beauty, her sweetness, the way everyone who saw her loved her. But no one ever saw her anymore.

Almost no one, that is. The queen was very busy and frequently traveled on mysterious business. As far as Jack knew, she had been troubled by recent hair loss. Which didn't make sense to him, because she still had as much hair as ever! (He should have asked for a spell-check.)

Whenever she got back, she checked in with Jack first thing. This particular time when she returned, he was nowhere to be found. She went out into the garden to ask Snow White where Jack was.

Snow White hung upside down from the branches of a tree, deep in the heavy shade it provided. Jack was digging in the vegetable patch with feverish devotion, even though it was Snow White's job.

"Jack," the queen said.

Jack continued digging.

"Jack, that is Snow White's chore. You don't know which vegetables to plant. You've never even willingly eaten a vegetable in your life. I don't think you could name a single one."

"I know," Jack said, voice distant and dreamy. "Isn't it wonderful that Snow White's letting me do it for her?"

The queen took Jack's face in her hands and tipped it up toward her own. Though Jack was normally healthy and tan, he looked pale today. Almost as fair as the queen.

"You!" she said, pointing to Snow White. "Get back to work!"

"That's not fair! You spoil him, and you're so mean to me!" Snow White hissed at Jack, lunging forward.

The queen grabbed Jack's hand and yanked him out of Snow White's grasp. Then the queen dragged him away from the garden, through the castle, and out the front gate. She tossed a bag of gold at him.

"Get out of here."

Jack's big eyes filled with tears. "What? Why?"

"Go to the first village in the next kingdom. There's a woman there, an old friend. Tell her I sent you. She'll look after you. She has a daughter your age—Jill, I think. You two will get along. And if that doesn't work out, keep going until you find another castle. Castles always have work."

"But we already have a castle! I want to stay here! With you! And with . . . Snow White." His eyes got far away and fuzzy again.

The queen kicked his bottom, startling him out of his trance. "And don't come back!" she shouted as he scurried away.

The villagers saw this and shook their heads. They muttered to each other about the wicked queen. If she treated her first stepson that way, how must she be treating poor Snow White?

Every morning, the queen dragged poor little Snow White out of her bed and into the sunny dressing room. Castles were very inefficient, and each room served only one purpose. A dressing room, for getting dressed. A dining room, for dining. A bathroom, for bathing. A ball room, for playing ball. A toilet room for . . . toileting.

In the dressing room, the queen would sit next to Snow White with a mirror and stare at their reflections as they combed their hair. The queen's hair, still thick and dark, now with strands of silver. And Snow White's, as black as a raven. Or perhaps a bat.

"Truthful mirror in my hand," the queen would say, looking carefully at their reflected faces, "who's the fairest in the land?"

And the queen was always satisfied that it was herself, not Snow White.

"Why don't you ever look me in the eyes?" Snow White asked one morning, her high voice as sweet as ice cream. If you listened to it too much, it gave you the same sort of brain freeze, too.

"Of course I look you in the eyes," the queen said, looking at Snow White's smooth forehead.

"No, you don't. You aren't right now."

"Of course I am," the queen said, looking at Snow White's perfect button nose.

Snow White began to cry and then ran away to her real mother's old room. She sat at the window, staring

out at the kingdom that should have been hers. She tried
to have a good attitude, but it just wasn't fair. Her stepmother was the worst. She made Snow White do all the
work while Jack got to play. And then she let Jack leave,
when Snow White was forbidden from setting foot outside the castle grounds. She always dressed Snow White
in cheery primary colors, ignoring the fact that Snow
White loved black the most. And even though
Snow White hated garlic and wanted to throw up at the
taste, her stepmother insisted on cooking everything
with it. Then there was the matter of her stepmother's
neck. It was always covered! She had even changed the
castle uniforms to turtlenecks before firing everyone.
No one likes turtlenecks! Especially not Snow White.
The wicked queen took away everything that made
Snow White happy.

Poor Snow White was lonely, and she was sad, and
she was tired and sick from being forced to work in the
sun so much.

And she was always, always thirsty.

She stood in the middle of her dead mother's room.
Nothing had been changed. (No one wanted anything
that had belonged to the creepy queen. The room was

covered in tapestries of bats and cluttered by pillows with stitched-on sayings like "Home Is Where the Blood Is.")

Snow White opened her mother's old trunk and pulled out the gowns one by one. Her mother, it turned out, had terrible taste in clothing. She wore entirely pastels with bows. So many bows. Snow White sighed, wishing her mother were here right now. Her mother would never treat her the way her stepmother did!

Surely there was something in here worth wearing, though. Something she could have to remind her of the woman who had truly understood her. Snow White's hand brushed against something cold and hard in the middle of the dresses. She closed her fingers around it and pulled it out. Metal clinked with dull tones. Snow White smiled, showing each of her perfect, tiny, sharp teeth.

"Thank you, Mother," she whispered.

The queen woke up aching and sore. She thought she must be coming down with a cold. She unlocked her door, then unlocked Snow White's. She stumbled to the kitchen. To her surprise, Snow White volunteered to make their customary breakfast of oatmeal and garlic.

(Lunch was tuna fish sandwiches and garlic. Dinner was pasta and garlic, with a side of garlic. The kitchen did not smell pleasant, and, frankly, neither did their breath.)

"It's a beautiful morning." Snow White's singsong voice was sweeter than the honey they never ate with their oatmeal.

"Yes, it is," the queen croaked. Her whole throat felt like it was on fire.

"You look like you don't feel well. Let me get us ready today!"

The queen let Snow White brush her hair. She did it so softly, and it felt wonderful. Rather than forcing her to go outside, the queen agreed to let Snow White stay in and read aloud to her.

She really did have a nice voice, the queen thought. Despite everything, she cared for the child. As long as the queen remained the fairest in the land, everything would be okay.

The next morning, the queen awoke even sicker. She felt like a hive of hot lava bees had stung her throat.

Once again, she stumbled to her door and unlocked it. But it was already unlocked. *That's strange*, she thought. She very clearly remembered locking it the night before. She always locked her door!

Brushing it off as a mistake due to her sickness, she unlocked Snow White's room (at least she had remembered that!) and was greeted with sympathy. The girl sang and chattered all day, fussing over the queen. But no matter how hard Snow White tried, the queen never looked her in the eyes. Still, Snow White was so attentive that by the time it was night, the queen was almost feeling better.

"See you in the morning!" Snow White chirped cheerily, black eyes bright with feverish intensity the queen could not see.

The queen nodded, patting her affectionately on the head. After locking the doors, the queen draped a small strand of red thread on the doorknob to her room.

When she awoke the next morning, she could barely move. Her head felt as heavy as a three-story-long snake and her eyes felt as fuzzy as a pig's chinny chin chin. When she tried to get up, every muscle screamed like a prince locked in a tower.

Her door was still locked. But the thread was on the floor.

Trembling, the queen took out her mirror and stumbled to Snow White's room. She unlocked the door to find Snow White looking happier and healthier than ever. But the girl's skin was as white as a blanket of fog.

"Truthful mirror in my hand," the queen whispered through her tortured throat—which she now saw had two tiny red marks on the side—"who's the fairest in the land?" She looked at her own reflection, as pale as death (who, being Death, can't ever get a tan but at least doesn't have to use sunblock), and then she looked at Snow White's reflection.

Or, rather, where Snow White's reflection was supposed to be.

Snow White stood right there, smiling. She was the most beautiful girl the queen had ever seen. More beautiful than the queen had ever been. More beautiful than anyone had ever been. Her reflection should have said the same thing.

But in the mirror, *nothing*.

The queen let out a single sob, finally looking Snow

White in the eyes. The girl's bloodred lips parted in a triumphant smile—and then the queen slammed the door in her face, locking it up tight again.

She leaned against it, trembling. After several shaking breaths, she had barely enough strength to drag and shove all the moveable furniture in front of the door. It took her too long, and then she was so exhausted she knew she couldn't do what had to come next.

So the queen called for her huntsman.

If you looked in the kingdom's dictionary under *bully*, the full definition was the huntsman's picture. As much as everyone hated the queen for the way she locked up Snow White, they hated the huntsman even more. They were both mean, but at least the queen was pretty. It was a very shallow kingdom, sadly.

"Hey, babe," the huntsman said.

"You do realize I'm the queen."

He grinned, winking. "Oh yeah, I do. Listen, what are you doing tonight? Maybe you and I could go out. On a date."

"Yuck."

"Okay, some other time, then. Is this about the snake? Still haven't found it."

The queen shook her head and pointed to Snow White's bedroom. "There is a wild animal in there. I need you to capture it, take it outside the village, and leave it in the meadow near the dark forest in the next kingdom. You'll need to do it before sunset. It's very important that you leave it in the middle of the meadow, directly in the sunlight."

"Got it. Dark forest. Midnight. Kill it."

"No!" The queen rubbed her forehead. The huntsman was like a headache in human form. "Meadow. Sunlight. Leave it."

"Okay!"

"I want you to repeat it back to me."

"Leave the sunlight in the meadow."

"No," the queen said, gritting her teeth. "How can you leave sunlight in a meadow? Take the *creature* to the *meadow* and leave it in the *sunlight*."

The huntsman groaned. "This is getting boring. I got it."

The queen pointed to a large bag made of thick, rough fabric. "Capture the animal and tie it up in that bag." Then the queen held out a strip of black cloth. "And you need to do it blindfolded."

The huntsman frowned at the blindfold, then looked warily from side to side. "Is this a trick? Am I being pranked?" He clapped his hands and bounced up and down on his massive, clunky feet. "No! It's a surprise party! I always wanted a surprise party! Every year I tell my friends they'd better throw me a surprise party or I'll beat them up. Then I punch them to make sure they understand." He paused, frowning. "And then by the time my birthday comes around, I don't have any friends. It's weird."

"No parties. You simply can't look at the creature. It's too dangerous. Can you do this or not?"

"Do you dare me to?"

The queen was beginning to seriously question her choice to use the huntsman. But she didn't have any other options. "Yes," she said, sighing heavily. "I dare you."

The huntsman was a little disappointed that it wasn't a party, but he loved a good dare. It was actually his greatest flaw: He was unable to refuse a dare. Because of this, the huntsman had only three remaining toes, no hair, and had not been able to taste anything for the last five years due to an incident with an industrial-size jar of ghost peppers. He also had an unfortunate tattoo on his arm that said LOVE MOME FORVER. When asked, he usually lied and said Mome Forver was his girlfriend. In truth, he just really loved his mom and had picked a terrible tattoo artist. (Another reason spelling matters.)

The queen tied the blindfold around his eyes as tightly as she could. Then she stuffed garlic in all his pockets. Finally, she shoved cotton into his ears so he couldn't hear anything.

"THIS IS THE WEIRDEST JOB I'VE EVER HAD," he shouted.

She ignored him. Taking a deep breath, she dragged aside the furniture, opened the door, and pushed him inside. Then she slammed the door shut and locked it again. There were some bumps, a few curses, and a terrible hiss and shriek.

"DONE!" the huntsman said, banging triumphantly on the door.

Relief wilted the queen like an old piece of lettuce. This was not the way she had wanted things to go. All her hard work and sacrifice! All that time spent looking in a mirror! Even sending away poor Jack.

But a stepmother had to do what a stepmother had to do. She squared her shoulders, opened the door, and let the huntsman out. The shape of poor Snow White wriggled in the bag, letting out inhuman shrieks.

The queen put one hand on the bag, a single tear in her eyes. But the queen couldn't let Snow White be the fairest in the land. It had to be done.

She pulled the blindfold off the huntsman.

"WHAT DO I DO NOW?" HE SHOUTED, BECAUSE HE COULDN'T HEAR ANYTHING AND DIDN'T REALIZE THE QUEEN COULD HEAR PERFECTLY WELL. THIS IS WHAT YOU DO, TOO, WHEN YOU HAVE HEADPHONES ON AND FORGET NO ONE ELSE DOES. SEE HOW ANNOYING IT IS?

Sighing in exasperation, the queen grabbed a quill and ink and scribbled instructions as quickly as she could. They were running out of time.

"Do not look at the creature. Do not listen to the creature. Take the bag to the meadow. Untie it and *leave it in the sun.*"

The huntsman took the note and nodded, smiling big to show off several chipped and missing teeth. He really did need to learn how to say no to dares. He also really, really needed to learn how to read. But he was too embarrassed to tell that to the pretty queen. So he took the note, slung the bag over his shoulder, and set off.

The queen stood in her tower, silently crying. Her time as queen was over. She'd go to the next kingdom and resume her work there. At least there was still some good she could do for others. She watched out the window as the huntsman carried Snow White out of the village and out of her life forever.

Or so she thought.

Meanwhile, Jack . . .

Jack and Jill went up the hill
to fetch a pail of water
She pushed him in and, with a grin,
went on to further slaughter.

Jill skipped home, then, all alone,
she traveled through the wood
And on her head, in crimson red,
she wore a velvet hood.

CHAPTER TWO

"The Princess and the ... Pea?"

Once upon the same time, in the other castle we saw at the beginning of the book—the one with a tower—a king and a queen had a rather musical problem.

They sat together on matching thrones. They were wrapped in silk and fur and dripping with jewels. Even though no one was there to see them, they acted *very* royal. Their spines were as straight as rulers because, as rulers, their spines could not possibly be any other way.

"How are we ever going to marry off our son? There aren't any good princesses anymore," the king said with a scowl.

"Back in my day," the queen said, holding a perfumed handkerchief beneath her nose because even the air wasn't fancy enough for her, "princesses were serious, proper things. Nowadays they're all insane."

"You can't get through a single conversation with them before they break into song!"

The queen nodded. "Just the other day I was trying to talk to a princess and she started singing midsentence! She kept pausing, like I should join in. How would I possibly know what to sing back? How does she even know the words? I had her thrown in the dungeon."

"As well you should have, my queen. I refuse to run a kingdom where everyone has to constantly be ready to break into a musical number. Think of the cost! All the lost hours of work. The shoes worn out by elaborate dance routines. Not to mention the voice lessons we'd have to buy. No singing princesses for us. I want a good old-fashioned, run-of-the-mill, needlework-loving princess."

"I want her to be stuffy and uptight. No enormous, sparkling eyes and exuberance for life. She should be frequently ill, look as though she always has a bad taste in her mouth, and be extremely delicate to the point of ridiculousness."

The king sighed, patting his large, velvet-clad belly. "Where will we find such a creature?"

"We should have a test. Perhaps some sort of obstacle course, and whichever princess throws the most proper tantrum over being asked to perform physical labor wins." The queen sighed, rubbing the deep, dark circles beneath her eyes. "I can't think of anything else. I'm too tired. There was a cricket outside last night, so I couldn't sleep."

"I didn't hear a cricket."

"Neither did I, but I was sure that *somewhere* out there a cricket was making noise, and it bothered me so much I didn't get any rest. You know how difficult it is for me to sleep."

It was true. She needed a mattress made from precisely 10,000 feathers of newborn geese. If the geese were teenagers, or there were 9,999 feathers, she could not sleep.

The room had to be exactly the temperature of a jellied eel dish. However, not one of the servants could decide at what temperature jellied eel could possibly taste good. So they had to constantly bring in ice and remove it, stoke the fire and smother it, and finally employ several handmaidens to sit at her bedside and gently blow on her face all night long. The handmaidens, of course, were permitted to eat nothing but honey so that their breath wasn't offensive.

For some reason, handmaidens kept quitting.

"My queen, I know what we should do! A true princess, one as royal as you, will be an equally sensitive sleeper. We shall invite them, one by one, to spend the night in our castle. And beneath their mattress we will place a single pea."

The queen gasped in horror. "Why, I won't be able to sleep for a week just imagining the discomfort!"

"Precisely! So if the princess comes out in the morning refreshed and alert, we'll know she's not a true enough princess for us."

The queen nodded, pinched eyes shining beneath her enormous crown. "And if she's exhausted and has not slept, we'll immediately marry her to our son!"

The king suddenly looked nervous. He darted his eyes around the imposing throne room, with its soaring ceilings and gold-trimmed pillars. Everything in there was fancy and breakable and flammable. It felt like a museum. It had not been a very fun place for the prince to grow up. And, even worse, every time the prince tried to sing a song about it, he was sent back to his tower. He had stopped singing, but ever since the unfortunate escape, they never let him out at all.

"Where *is* our son?" the king asked, sweat beading on his wrinkled forehead.

The queen jingled a large ring of keys fastened to the gold belt around her waist. "Don't worry. We're safe. There's no reason to consult him. We'll surprise him when we've found him the perfect wife."

(In fact, the poor prince does not appear in this story at all. Which, given that it is entirely about finding him a wife, is rather mysterious, isn't it? Why do they keep him in that tower? Hmmm . . .)

The king sighed with relief, snatching the queen's nose handkerchief to wipe his brow. She pulled another out of her dress, glaring at him. "Now that one will need to be burned."

They both cringed at the word *burned*, then cleared their throats and stared royally at nothing. It was their greatest skill as rulers.

The first princess arrived on a Tuesday.

Tuesdays are the most disagreeable day of the week. Fridays are always welcome. They're like your friend who has the best jokes and shares treats at lunch. Thursdays try to overcompensate to get you to like them more than Fridays. Their jokes are never as good as Fridays', but at least they try. Saturdays and Sundays are like your favorite cousins who come to stay and there's a sleepover and everything is super fun. Mondays are like your mom after your cousins leave. She's tired and cranky because the whole house is a mess, but at least you had a good time. And Wednesdays squat in the middle, balancing everything, ready to tip from the dull beginning of the week into the inevitable slide into the weekend.

But Tuesdays! Tuesdays are the bullies of the week. Last weekend is a distant memory; next weekend is still too far away to look forward to. And if everyone is still tired from Monday? Tuesday doesn't care! Tuesday will kick you right in the stomach and laugh all the way until next week, when it does it again.

The queen, being very disagreeable herself, felt a special kinship with Tuesdays. She thought it appropriate that the princess chose that day to arrive, and took it as a very good sign.

The princess was small, with a pointed nose and squinty eyes. She resembled a rat who had been dressed in brown silk and weighed down with gold. But at least she was like a normal rat and not an albino one, so her eyes weren't red. This isn't as scary as Snow White's story. I'm glad.

While the princess was eating supper—and complaining about every course, a fact that filled the king and queen with hope—the king took their new servant boy, Jack, aside.

"You've prepared the room?"

"Yup."

"And the pea? You didn't forget the pea."

Jack nodded with a pained look on his face. "I took care of that. But I still don't understand why you wanted me to do it."

The king sniffed haughtily. "Of course you wouldn't understand. Which is why you are a servant and I am the king. Now go and make the pease porridge for the rest of the servants to eat. You can eat the scraps from the princess's plate."

"*What* kind of porridge??" Jack asked.

"Pease porridge! It's the least we can do for our servants. No, really, it's the very least we can do to keep them alive."

Jack shrugged and did as he was told. This whole job thing was weird. He didn't much like it, but it was better than being shoved in a well.

After dinner, the king and the queen sat in the library with the princess. She complained about the journey from her kingdom.

She complained about the height and width of the stairs to the castle, which she felt were several centimeters from what the ideal height and width of stairs should be. She was very passionate about stairs, as it turned out.

She complained about the color of the flames in the fireplace, which she thought should be rather more yellow than orange. She disliked the color orange in general, which she found offensive and thought should be banned.

And she complained about the prince, whom they had not invited to come down.

The king and queen were very encouraged. They complained about the prince constantly, and they had known him since he was born. So for her to complain about him before meeting him was an indication that she was *very* intelligent. She seemed just about perfect!

When they sent the princess off to bed, they were giddy with excitement. All she had to do was pass the pea test, and they would have a wife for their son!

The king and queen were dressed and sitting on their thrones bright and early the next morning, waiting to give the princess the good news.

"I couldn't sleep at all last night, imagining a pea beneath my mattress!" the queen said. "I am so tired and grouchy, I will probably sentence a peasant to life in prison today for no reason at all."

The king smiled proudly. "And soon we will have a daughter-in-law every bit as wonderful as you."

The princess stormed into the throne room, hair askew, squinty face twisted up into a ratty expression of fury. A furious rat is something no one ever wants to behold, much less first thing in the morning. Even calm rats are preferably avoided, unless they are your pets. But you wouldn't want one for a daughter-in-law.

However, in this case, the king and queen were delighted.

"How did you sleep?" the king asked, giggling as he had not done since he was a little boy and had his tutor whipped for telling him four times two wasn't ten.

"Yes, how did you sleep?" the queen asked, smiling in a way she thought was benevolent, but that would have made a small child—or even a small adult—cry.

"I thought your stairs were bad, but they were nothing compared to that room! I have never been so horrendously treated in my entire life. If I never set foot in this castle again, it will be too soon!"

The king and queen turned to each other, clasping hands. "We did it!" they exclaimed. "We got a princess with high standards and no musical ability whatsoever!"

They turned back to inform the princess that she had passed their test and would marry their son—

Only to find she had already left the throne room. They cringed as she slammed every single door on her way out. It was a very large castle, with forty-one doors between the princess and the outer gate.

It took a very long time.

"Well," the king said, frowning. "Perhaps she was *too* sensitive."

The queen sat on the throne with a huff. The princess was obviously more sensitive than even she was, which made the queen *very* angry. But the queen couldn't very well storm out of her own castle and slam all her own doors. It was very unfair. She comforted herself with the thought that at least slamming doors was an unqueenly thing to do. She could injure one of her precious, royal hands.

She would have a servant do it for her!

She rang the bell for a servant, but it took several minutes before one finally appeared. He was out of breath, with his cap nearly falling off. It was Jack, again.

"Why did it take you so long? Why wasn't someone here sooner?"

Jack shrugged. "A few servants didn't come in today. We're all doing double duty. The head maid is mucking the stables, the butler is weeding the garden, and the cook is cleaning toilets."

"The cook is cleaning toilets?" the king asked, horrified. "Well, have her hands removed before she goes back to cooking for us!"

Jack scratched his head beneath his cap. "You mean have her hands washed?"

"No! I mean have her hands removed. I won't have hands that touch the toilets touch my food."

"But . . . if she doesn't have any hands, how can she . . ."

"Enough!" the king roared. "Send for the next princess!"

The queen waved her perfumed handkerchief. "And as soon as you've done that, slam every door in the castle!"

The first princess had arrived on a Tuesday, but the second princess *acted* like a Tuesday. She walked in with an escorting guard on either side of her royal person and looked the king and queen up and down.

"Oh," she said. "What an . . . *interesting* crown." Even though she was smiling, the way she said *interesting* felt like being pinched.

The king's hand darted to his crown, fondling the golden prongs. "It's an heirloom."

"Oh," she said. "So it's *sentimental*. That explains why you'd wear something that ugly." She smiled again, like what she had said was nice. Her face was so blank it was like a mirror, so the king and queen smiled back to reflect her. They were pretty sure she was insulting them, but she said it so sweetly and with such a bland smile it was confusing.

They ate supper with her.

"Is that a painting of the prince?" she asked, looking at the royal portraits glowering in a long line along the wall. The most recent was, in fact, the prince. It had been painted through bars and at a distance, but the painter mostly got his face right. Though the artist had, at the queen's request, made the prince look haughty and dour instead of clueless and pleasant. And the artist had also given him eyebrows again. Big bushy ones, like two mutant caterpillars. I prefer him without eyebrows.

The queen smiled fondly at the grimacing portrait. "Yes, that is him."

"Oh," said the princess. "He has your . . . *nose.*" She slid that smile onto the end of the sentence again, but the queen felt the words pinching her.

The queen put her hand over her nose. She had always thought she had a wonderful nose—large and noble, like an eagle. But now she wondered if eagles were not the standard of beauty for women.

The queen excused herself early. She summoned Jack the servant.

"Is her room prepared, the pea in place?" She paced, out of sorts and wishing she could somehow cover up her nose.

"Yes." Jack shook his head. "I still don't understand why you would want me to do that to the bed, though."

"Don't question me," the queen snapped.

Later, she sat in front of a mirror looking at her nose from every possible angle and being upset at each of them.

"I think she is an amazing princess," the queen said to the king, who was trying to make his tummy look smaller. The princess had asked in an innocent tone whether large stomachs were fashionable in this kingdom, because they certainly weren't in hers.

"You do?" the king asked.

"A queen should make everyone else feel inferior, and she is certainly skilled at that."

"She is," the king agreed.

Even though the second princess had such a marvelous queenly quality, the king and queen were both nervous the next morning. Would her skills at finding fault extend to the pea in the mattress?

In place of the princess, though, they were met by Jack. He carried a letter. It was neatly rolled and tied with an elegant bow.

Dear King and Queen,

While I'm certain your son is as lovely as your castle, I'm afraid neither is to my taste. Thank you so much for your overwhelming hospitality.

All best,
Princess Tuesday

"Is it just me," said the king, "or do some of these words feel like she's pinching us?"

The queen rubbed her rear end. "It isn't just you. I don't understand! Why did she leave?"

"She must have felt the pea! But why couldn't she have stayed until she found out the good news? We've lost another one." The king drooped sorrowfully.

The queen wouldn't admit it, but she was relieved. If the first princess was more sensitive than she was, the second was certainly more critical than she was. And the queen did not like the idea of a daughter-in-law who was better than her.

Jack, still standing there because he hadn't been dismissed, shifted awkwardly from foot to foot. "Maybe it's the bed? It doesn't seem very pleasant."

"Oh, what would you know!" the queen growled. She looked Jack up and down, trying to find some way to make him feel bad about himself. "You're just—you have—isn't your face *interesting*?"

Jack brightened, smiling and standing straighter. "Thank you! My stepmother always told me so, too. She said an interesting face is better than a handsome one, because handsome faces don't always mean handsome hearts, but interesting faces always mean interesting minds."

The queen slumped in her throne, even her ruler's spine wilted with disappointment. Jack obviously did not feel one bit bad about himself. "Oh, go eat the princess's breakfast since she isn't here. And then make the pease porridge for the other servants!"

"Can't I make them something else?" Jack asked.

"Go now, or I'll have you thrown in the dungeon!"

"There aren't even enough servants to eat it! We still have leftovers from the last batch."

"Then take the leftovers to the village and let the peasants eat it! They'll be grateful."

"I don't think they will . . ." Jack muttered. But he did as he was told. He'd leave a batch for that rotten Jill, at least. It was the least he could do.

The third princess was their last hope. The princess from the next castle over was missing. (Poor, beautiful Snow White!) Every other princess in the area had rosy cheeks and massive eyes. They even *looked* like singers. It was the third princess, or none.

She arrived in the throne room without the customary two guards. She was even smaller than the first princess but decidedly less Tuesday-ish than the second one. The third princess looked like nothing so much as a detention, a time-out, or a grounding of epic proportion.

"Where are my soldiers?" the king asked, standing in a rage. "They aren't doing their duty!"

"I had them thrown in the dungeon," the princess said.

"You . . . what?"

"I didn't like the way the first one smelled. And the second one almost smiled when my foot caught on a loose tile. He was definitely thinking about smiling. So I had them thrown in the dungeon."

"But that's my job!" the queen said.

The princess narrowed her eyes. "It's very improper to speak to a princess before you have been introduced."

The king and queen, thoroughly embarrassed, introduced themselves.

Supper was late. The cook, no longer having hands, had a hard time managing the meals. The princess had her thrown in the dungeon, along with the two servers.

"But you can't have them locked up," the king protested.

"The soup was cold, and the jellied eel tasted too much of jelly and eel."

"Yes," the queen agreed, "but what he means is, this is our castle. You can't go throwing our servants into our dungeon."

The princess narrowed her eyes. "I don't like being disagreed with. I'm certain there's more room in the dungeon."

"Guards!" the queen screeched. "Someone! Anyone! Escort the princess to her room!"

Jack hurried into the dining hall.

"Don't we have any other servants?" the king asked, frowning.

"Almost all of them are sick. Or in the dungeon." Jack looked warily at the princess.

"Is the princess's room ready? Did you . . . specially prepare it?" The queen was terrified that this princess would notice the pea, but she was more terrified to tell the princess to go home. Not only because she was their last chance, but also because she didn't want the princess to get angry with her. And, after the more sensitive first princess, the second princess making everyone feel bad about themselves, and now this princess being better at throwing people in the dungeon, the queen was starting to wonder if she had *any* special talents, after all.

(I think the queen is a little off on her princessy priorities, but I hate being thrown in dungeons, so I'm not going to tell her so.)

Jack, who also hated being thrown in dungeons, nodded uneasily. "I did what you asked."

"Good. Take her to her room. I hope you sleep . . . well?" The king looked at the queen, and she shrugged. She didn't know what she wanted, either.

They didn't have to wait until morning.

No sooner had Jack escorted the princess to her room than she came roaring back into the throne room.

"What is the meaning of this? I have never been so insulted in all my life!"

The queen tried to smile. "Was the mattress uncomfortable, dear?"

"Uncomfortable! It was disgusting!"

The king's mouth trembled as he, too, tried to force a smile. "Good news! That means you are worthy of marrying our—"

"Into the dungeon with both of you!" the princess screamed, pointing at them.

Everyone stood there.

"Um," Jack said, "they're the king and queen. You can't throw them into the dungeon."

"I can and I will! I'll throw *all* of you in the dungeon for this!"

"But don't you want to marry our son?" the queen asked, wringing her hands in despair. She didn't want to go to the dungeon. She didn't have any good dungeon outfits, and she was certain it wouldn't smell nice. Plus, she probably wasn't the most popular person down there.

"After what you've done to me? You're lucky I don't have you all executed! Now where are the guards?"

"You had them thrown in the dungeon," the king said, waving his hands in exasperation.

The princess narrowed her eyes and everyone froze, bowing their heads meekly. Someday, the princess would make an excellent mother, school principal, or dictator. Maybe all three. "Very well. I'm having your *entire kingdom* thrown in the dungeon."

Jack couldn't figure out how that would work. "Are you actually *throwing* people into the dungeon? Who do you have to do it? They'd have to be pretty strong to toss around so many people. And nobody could lift a whole kingdom! Do you mean everyone in the kingdom, or the kingdom itself? Because there's no way the actual kingdom with all the buildings and animals and dirt would fit in the dungeon."

"I don't mean I'll put the kingdom in the actual dungeon, you idiot! I mean a metaphorical dungeon!"

Jack scratched his head. "I don't think you can make bars out of metaphors."

"Argh!" the princess screamed, stomping one tiny, terrible foot. "I will go to every kingdom in the land and tell them all what you have done. No one—NO ONE—will ever visit here again. And no one will ever be allowed to leave! You are all GROUNDED FOREVER!"

With that she turned and thundered from the castle.

"All over one little pea." The king took off his crown

and rubbed his bald head. "I thought we were sensitive, but apparently princesses these days are even harder to please."

"You did put just *one* pea under the mattress, right?" the queen asked.

Jack scrunched up his face in confusion. "I don't know that you could say 'just one.' You can't really measure it that way."

"What do you mean? Of course you can measure a single pea."

"I guess, but it all depends on how much I had to drink that afternoon."

The king frowned. "What does you drinking have to do with putting a pea under a mattress?"

"Well, I can't very well do it if I don't have to go to the bathroom."

The queen's eyes widened as the full, horrible truth descended on her in a flush. I mean, a rush.

No. I mean a *flush*.

"Jack," she said. "Spell *pea*."

"Well, that's easy. There's only one way. P-E-E."

(I told you spelling matters.)

The queen pointed a trembling finger at the door.

"You've ruined everything, you disgusting, vile creature! Go to the dungeon!"

"But I did what you told me! And the dungeon is full!"

"GET OUT!" the queen screamed. "JUST GET OUT."

Jack, confused and disappointed at once again being kicked out of a castle, ran as fast as he could.

"But who will make the pease porridge now?" the king asked. "Jack has been cooking it for all the servants!"

"Oh no," the queen whispered. "*Pease* porridge. He didn't . . ."

Oh NO.

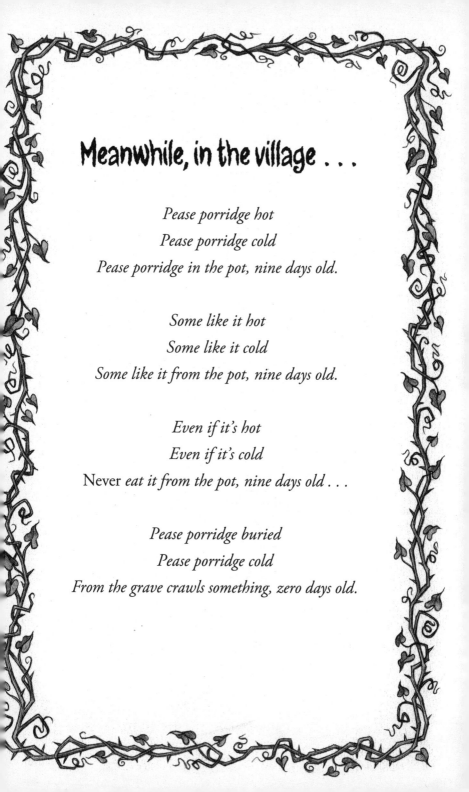

Meanwhile, in the village . . .

Pease porridge hot
Pease porridge cold
Pease porridge in the pot, nine days old.

Some like it hot
Some like it cold
Some like it from the pot, nine days old.

Even if it's hot
Even if it's cold
Never *eat it from the pot, nine days old . . .*

Pease porridge buried
Pease porridge cold
From the grave crawls something, zero days old.

CHAPTER THREE

"Little Dead Riding Hood"

Once upon that same time, a little girl went into the woods.

Little girls go into the woods all the time. They go there to pick berries or to dangle their feet in cool, clear streams. They go there to play hide-and-seek, though they can't say who they are hiding from or what they are seeking. They go there to make a burrow for themselves and find special hidden places where they think they could maybe live forever. Little girls go into the woods because the woods are wild places, and little girls are told they must never be wild.

But the woods like wild things, and so little girls like the woods. Woods keep the secrets that adults force little girls to have. And many little girls know, deep in their darkest heart space where no one else can ever see, something no one else does:

They are actually monsters.

There's nothing wrong with that. But it can be hard to be a monster when everyone tells you that you are the opposite. All the monster parts of you—the anger, the wildness, the hunger for *more*—are parts you have to keep hidden.

And so little girls go into the woods. Sometimes they leave their little heart monsters behind in their burrows in the woods, and come out again to grow up and be exactly what they are told they are.

Sometimes they are consumed by their little heart monsters and never really come out of the woods again. People cluck their tongues and whisper about the trag-edy, but they don't really mind because there are enough nice, quiet, proper little girls to comfort them.

But sometimes, a little girl goes into the woods with a secret heart monster, and she comes back out a mon-ster with a secret little girl heart.

I think those are the best kind, don't you?

And at this particular time, in this particular forest, the little girl going into the woods wore a long red cloak. It fastened with a ribbon bow around her neck, and had a hood that went up over her hair and draped her face in deep shadows. She loved that hood. It made her feel mysterious. Peering out through it at the world, she pretended she carried secrets in her basket.

What she actually carried was far more boring than secrets. Some bread, some cold chicken, a bit of cake, a cork-topped glass bottle of lemonade, and some porridge from the stupid castle. Surely a castle could send better food than porridge.

"Now, Jill, take it straight to your grandmother," her mother had sternly cautioned. "Stay on the path. And no dillydallying about! You are still in a lot of trouble for what you did to Jack, young lady."

The little girl pulled her cloak down lower over her face. Jack hadn't gotten in trouble for kicking her out of her own bed and making her sleep on the floor. Jack never got in trouble for climbing on things, or shouting, or knocking all the heads off the flowers with a stick. Jack never got in trouble for bragging or spitting or pushing.

She was not one bit sorry for pushing him into the well. And that was part of why she was being punished so much. You and I know that parents want to see that you feel bad for what you did. If she could have worked up some remorseful tears or written a flowery apology letter, she would probably have been off the hook. But she just couldn't do it.

She was always in trouble anyway, for something ridiculous like talking too loud, or eating too much, or laughing too brightly. Even her face got her in trouble for looking too smart, or too mean, or too sullen.

She liked being *too*. She didn't want to stop.

Her stomach growled. She growled back at it.

And then the woods growled, too.

Startled, she stopped. The path stretched ahead of her. It was clear and precise, bordered by a heavy wall of trees on both sides. The branches crowded overhead, clawing at the sky over the path. The trees seemed to hint that they would love to grab the path and drag it away. And the little girl thought she'd like the woods better with no path.

The little girl looked to her right. The gloom of the forest hung heavy and green, impenetrable after a few feet. But, over to the left, past snaking roots and between massive trunks, the sun broke through to illuminate a small clearing filled with flowers. A large flat rock was in the center. Nature had prepared for a picnic.

"Don't ever leave the path," her mother cautioned in her memory. "It's *too dangerous*."

But the little girl liked *too*.

She clambered over the roots, tugging her cloak free when it snagged on a branch. She could still see the path from the clearing. She was still safe.

Or so she thought.

She seated herself on the flat rock, then took out her grandmother's food and examined it. The cake couldn't be eaten without leaving evidence. She had no fork, and bite marks would show. Same with the chicken. It was so neatly sliced that even tearing a piece off would be obvious. The bread was a whole loaf, which would also give away her crime.

She was really very angry with her mother.

But the porridge . . .

She didn't have a spoon. The porridge was a big glop in a bowl with a cover on it. She stuck her finger in the middle experimentally. When she pulled it out, the porridge slowly settled back to fill it in.

(Oh dear. Please don't, little girl.)

She smiled, took a huge handful, and shoved it in her mouth.

(I feel a bit sick, don't you? I wish she knew what we know about that porridge.)

It was . . . not good. Really not good. (So much worse than not good, poor thing.) She gagged, but she had eaten it so fast she accidentally swallowed some. She thought it must have gone bad, which would explain why the castle had given it out for free.

Angry that her rebellious picnic had been ruined, she slammed the lid back on the bowl. She couldn't even open the lemonade to try to get the taste out of her mouth. So she was understandably quite annoyed when a wolf stepped into the clearing with a growling sneer.

"What do you want?" she snapped.

The wolf was taken aback. He was not used to that sort of greeting. "Augh!" he got a lot. "Oh no!" was quite common. "Watch out for the arghhguggleunghhhhh" was one of his favorites. But "What do you want?" was not something he had a ready answer for.

"That isn't how a little girl says hello, now, is it?" the wolf asked in his friendliest voice. It was about as friendly as a chain saw, but he *did* try.

"Well, I'm a little girl, and it's how I said hello, so I guess it is exactly how a little girl says hello." She crossed her arms and glared at the wolf. He was long and lean, with a great bushy tail and large yellow eyes.

He laughed. It sounded like the garbage disposal catching on a spoon. And when he finished laughing, he licked his big, sharp teeth. They were nearly as yellow as his eyes. "I suppose you are right. What's your name?"

The little girl did not want to tell him her name. She didn't even particularly like her name. The only thing her mother had ever given her that she liked was her cloak. So she said, "My name is Red Riding Hood."

The wolf laughed again. It was not meant to be a joke, and Red Riding Hood was indignant. Also, her stomach was beginning to hurt.

"Well, Little Red Riding Hood, where are you off to on this fine day?"

"I'm going to visit my grandmother."

The wolf's eyes widened and his tongue lolled out, long and delicately pink. He was a very lean wolf, as I had mentioned. And he was hungry. Very, very hungry. For some reason all the little animals in the forest had been missing lately. And he kept finding odd tracks on the ground, like something . . . slithering around. He had never eaten people before, but he was getting desperate. *One little girl would make a fine meal, but one little girl and one grandmother would make a better one, don't you think?*

Well, I hope *you* don't think so. You shouldn't be eating little girls or grandmothers. It was a rhetorical question the wolf was asking himself, so you shouldn't answer it. But *he* definitely did think so.

"And where does your grandmother live?" he asked.

Red Riding Hood gestured irritably down the path. "That way." Her stomach felt very bad now, and it was starting to radiate outward. She thought she might throw up, but she didn't want to do it with an audience. Especially a wolf audience.

"Listen," she said, annoyed and in pain. "Are you going to eat me? Because I think I'm going to be sick and I don't want to sit around chatting." She took out the glass lemonade bottle and smashed the bottom off against the rock. It left a jagged edge, and she held it between herself and the wolf's teeth. Her mother would have said it was too aggressive.

The wolf considered it. He could almost certainly still win. He was a monster, after all, and she was just a little girl.

But it wasn't ideal. If he ate Little Red Riding Hood now, he'd have a very full stomach. That would make the run to her grandmother's house decidedly uncomfortable. And she might succeed in injuring him, which was something predators avoid at all costs. He really wished she were just a little girl like she was supposed to be, instead of too much more.

But the old woman was in a nice, comfy house, and she was expecting a visitor. So she would be very likely to open the door without a fuss. He could eat her at his leisure, and then have a cushy resting place while he awaited Little Red Riding Hood.

And Little Red Riding Hood certainly wouldn't be armed when she went into her beloved grandmother's house.

The wolf sat on his haunches and scratched

innocently at his ear with his back paw. "Oh, no, I would never eat such an ill-mannered little girl. You're much too feisty for me."

"I like being *too*," Red Riding Hood grumbled.

"Have a lovely day." The wolf swept his head low like he was bowing to her, and then trotted off into the trees. As soon as Little Red Riding Hood could no longer see him, he changed direction.

You know where he's going and what he'll do when he gets there, so let's stay to keep poor, sick Red Riding Hood company.

Red Riding Hood leaned over and threw up, splattering the stone that had been such a charming picnic table.

Well, gross. On second thought, let's skip forward a bit.

Hmm. She's still throwing up.

Still . . . wait, no, I think she's done now!

Oh dear, I spoke too soon.

Skipping forward a bit more, Little Red Riding Hood was back on the path where she should have been all along. She stumbled instead of skipped now. Her sour stomach had turned to a sort of icy numbness that was spreading through her whole body. Sweat plastered her hair to her forehead beneath her cloak, and she shivered.

It was all she could do to put one foot in front of the other. She had even forgotten the picnic basket, left behind in the clearing. Her thoughts were sluggish and unfocused. *Grandma's house*, she repeated to herself over and over. She knew she needed to get to Grandma's house, and then things would be okay.

She was too tired, and too sick, and too woozy to think of anything else. She didn't like these *too*s at all.

She had been shambling along without paying attention to where she was, and her grandmother's house appeared in front of her so quickly that she bumped into the door. But now that she was here, she remembered she wanted to go inside.

She knocked.

"Come in," a rough voice called. Something about it was wrong, but in her hazy, sick brain she couldn't quite figure out what it was. So she opened the door and went inside.

The house was dim, all the shutters closed. The fire was out, too. If Red Riding Hood weren't so sick, she would know that meant something was wrong. Her grandmother liked to keep the cottage a few degrees below roasting. Once, a chicken wandered in from the yard, and by the time it walked to the table, it was almost fully cooked.

But Red Riding Hood was cold. Very cold. She kept her cloak on.

"Come here, my child," a voice crooned from her grandmother's bed, which took up the whole center of the cottage.

It was so dark, and her eyes weren't working quite right. But Red Riding Hood knew, deep in the part of her brain that was still functioning, that something was . . . different. Grandmother had always been thin and tiny, but now her body stretched too far beneath the cover of her quilt. Her knit cap fit strangely, with two large ears sticking out. And she held the blanket up over her nose and mouth.

But it wasn't the way her grandmother looked that was so troubling. It was that tantalizing smell . . .

"Why, Grandma," Red Riding Hood said, her voice low and creaking like old rotting wood crunching beneath a foot, "what big eyes you have."

"The better to see you with, my dear."

"Why, Grandma," Red Riding Hood said, her mouth beginning to water for some reason, "what big ears you have." She shuffled forward until she hit the edge of the bed.

"The better to hear you with, my dear." Her "grand-mother" let out that garbage-disposal laugh, then covered it up by pretending to cough. Very soon the wolf knew Red Riding Hood would comment on his teeth, and then he'd get to be clever *and* well-fed. This was the best day of his life.

"Why, Grandma," Red Riding Hood said, leaning much too close over the bed, "what delicious brains you have."

"The better to—wait, *what*?" The wolf sat up, dropping the blanket. "No, that's not what you're supposed to say. You're supposed to notice my teeth, and then I'm going to say, 'The better to eat you with,' and then you'll scream that delightful little-girl scream, and I'll gobble you up."

"Gobble," Red Riding Hood said, a thin stream of drool escaping her mouth.

"Yes, that's right, I'm going to eat you, but first I'd like—"

"Eat you," Red Riding Hood said.

"Yes, I know, you can stop repeating everything I say, it's getting annoying."

"Eat you," Red Riding Hood said again. Her hood fell back and a shiver went down the wolf's spine.

He swallowed nervously. "My, little girl, what red eyes you have."

Red Riding Hood said nothing.

"My, little girl, what gray skin you have."

Red Riding Hood said nothing.

"My, little girl, what sharp nails you have."

Red Riding Hood said nothing.

"My, little girl, what strong teeth you have!"

The better to eat you with, my dear, I say as we turn away from the horrific scene of gore and gorging that followed. But you can still hear a wolfish scream cut short, bones crunched, and finally, the particular squelching sound a brain makes when it is being eaten.

The front door burst open. A tall, strong woodsman stood, framed in the light, with an ax at his side. "I'm here to save you!" he shouted.

He rushed to the bedside and grabbed Little Red Riding Hood, carrying her out of the house and setting her on the ground. "You shouldn't be in the woods! Little girls don't belong out here." He posed, hands on hips, the sunlight behind him lighting his lustrous hair in shining chestnut shades. He looked like an advertisement for paper towels. She didn't seem to appreciate it, and he frowned, annoyed. "And you should smile when I talk to you, and say 'thank you.' I saved you."

It was then that he noticed she had bitten him. He

87

scrambled away from her, looking in horror at the no-longer-secret monster she was. "But you're just a little girl!" he shouted. "This can't be happening!"

People are always underestimating little girls in the woods. He ran back in to pick up the ax, but his steps got slow and heavy as the bite mark throbbed and turned cold.

It was already too late.

Little Dead Riding Hood still loved *too*.

Meanwhile, on a wall . . .

Humpty Dumpty sat on the wall,
Humpty Dumpty had a great fall,
All the king's horses and all the king's men,
Were nowhere to be found because they were
shambling across the countryside looking for
brains and couldn't be bothered to deal with
some strange egg-man's woes.

CHAPTER FOUR

"Cinders and Ashes"

Back at the castle, Jack had left in such disgrace, the king and queen were in a quandary. A *quandary* is sort of like a *quarry*, if instead of rocks you mined problems and troubles. And there was no way out. And it was slowly filling with water. Or, worse, pease porridge.

They had no servants left. Everyone was either in the dungeons thanks to the last princess, or had called in sick and then never come back. (They didn't have phones, of course, but they had messenger pigeons. The last few notes they had gotten were "too sick," "really too sick," and, most puzzling of all, "arrrrrrgggggghhhhhh.")

The queen sat on her throne. Her hair, normally teased and curled and primped for several hours each morning, hung limply. Her face, normally teased and curled and primped for several hours each morning, also hung limply. She couldn't figure out how to dress herself. She'd never done it before! She didn't know how to tie a knot or a bow, so this morning she was wrapped in a golden tablecloth. She couldn't even move her arms, which were pinned to her sides.

The king was far worse off. He couldn't stand up. Every time he tried, his velvet pants fell all the way to the floor. And though his underwear was expensive, he still didn't want everyone to see it. (It had miniature knights riding pink unicorns. He really loved unicorns. It's the only thing I can agree with him on.)

All this was bad enough. But with no servants, there was no one to take care of the prince. The king and queen both looked with dread toward the door to the tower where they kept him.

"We have to do something," the queen said.

"We do," the king agreed.

"Have you heard back from the stepmother I wanted to hire?"

The king sighed. "She was interested, until she found

out that you were still alive. Apparently that disqualifies us from needing a stepmother."

"It's not my fault I'm still alive!"

The king patted her hand. "I know, my dear. She was being very unreasonable."

The queen slumped in her chair. She had always considered herself an exclamation mark, but now she knew it was because her corsets had been so tight she had no other choice. Without a corset, she was like a comma. She hated commas! They dragged everything out, linking one thought to the next, making sentences longer, and longer, and longer, until you didn't even know where the sentence started or why you were still reading it, because the stupid writer kept putting in commas instead of ending the sentence like a sane, normal, pleasant person would, and now she was a comma instead of an exclamation point, the forceful end of a sentence, which made her feel like her life was nothing but a pause, followed by a pause, with no end in

Well. You get what she felt like.

"We need a princess," the king said.

"There are no princesses!"

"Maybe if we were less picky? I could . . . handle some singing. A little. Now and then." He grimaced, looking like a toad. That look was helped by the fact that he was wearing several green cushions glued to his waist instead of a shirt.

"I would take a singing princess, too, but we can't! The last princess meant it when she said our whole kingdom is grounded. She built a wall of magic vines around every-thing. No one can get in. And we can't get out." The queen was very bitter about this. It was brilliant and mean. She should have thought of it herself as punishment for someone else! Oh, that horrible, wonderful princess. She was going to make the best queen ever someday. (Actually, the princess would assume the title of Supreme Mother Principal Dictator. We were right about her!)

"Forget princesses, then!" the king said. "We just need a wife for him. Any wife."

"Preferably someone with cleaning skills." The queen eyed several dust bunnies in the corner that were grow-ing to be more like dust wildebeests.

"How will we choose?"

"Throw a party!" she said. Her stomach growled angrily. "A potluck party." Even Jack, that horrible idiot who had ruined everything, had left them. Not that she would have eaten anything he cooked, but still. "We should make it a ball. All those long dresses will sweep the floor. And if we invite everyone in the whole kingdom, surely there will be *someone* willing to marry our son."

The king made a strangled noise of disapproval. Think of the noise your mom makes when she picks up the socks you've been wearing for the last week without washing them. Sort of like that.

The queen bit her lip. Normally her lips were painted red, but she didn't know how to use her own makeup. Today she had put mascara on them, and her lips did look very full and long! And also black. "You're right. We can't have a normal courtship. They'll figure out the truth. I know! We'll let him pick. And whoever he picks has to marry him. Immediately."

"It will work," the king said, looking nervously at the locked door that led to the tower that led to their son.

"It has to work," the queen whispered.

Meanwhile, in that same kingdom, it was a dark and stormy night.

Other than the fact that it was the middle of a bright and sunny day. Cinderella just *wished* it were a dark and stormy night. Then they would have to light a fire.

Mmm, a fire . . .

She hummed happily to herself, combing through the ashes in the fireplace. Maybe this time there would be an ember left. Even a single spark. She could do so much with a single spark.

"Ella!" her stepmother said with a voice like a bucket of water being dumped on her head.

"It's *Cinder*ella," one of her two stepsisters said. She had a very small face on a very large head. It was the opposite of how baby animals look. It was also the opposite of how cute baby animals are. This stepsister always followed Cinderella around, bossing her, telling her what to do and not to do.

"If *Ella*," her stepmother said, glaring, "has time to poke around in the ashes, she obviously needs more to do. Go make lunch, Ella. Then you can polish the floors."

When Cinderella's father had been alive, she had never been treated like this. He went away on his trips and came back with the most wondrous gifts. New clothes and jewelry, magnifying glasses, and, best of all, books! Books with their pages of dry paper. So much paper . . .

She was never allowed to have books now.

Singing a soft, sad song to herself, Cinderella made lunch. Cold cucumber sandwiches, cold tea, cold pudding. She longed for something toasty and comforting. But her stepmother wouldn't allow anything warm.

When they were finished eating, she cleaned. Then she cleaned. Then she cleaned some more. It didn't matter how clean the house was, her stepmother always found another task. Today, she was polishing the backs of the tiles in the kitchen floor. First, she had to pry up the tile. Then she polished the back. Then she re-glued it onto the floor.

Does anyone ever see the backs of tiles? No. But at least this wasn't as bad as the time her stepmother had her take inventory of the feathers on each chicken out in the coop. At least tiles didn't peck or scratch. Or poo.

At the end of every day, when Cinderella was too tired to see straight, her stepmother walked her up to the tower. (As you have noticed, there were a lot of towers in this kingdom. It all started a long time ago with the very first king. He was terrified of rain. So he had towers built everywhere, and then found all the tallest people in the kingdom. He made them stand at the tops of the towers. That way, they'd know the second it started raining, and could send a messenger pigeon with a warning. But by the time the pigeon got to the king, the rain had already hit the ground. Kings aren't kings because they're smart. But it explains why the zoning laws allow such high towers. You can write the kingdom council to have them revise the rules, but it'll take three years for them to write back.)

"Goodnight, Ella," the stepmother said every night, after checking every corner of the room to make sure Cinderella hadn't managed to hide anything precious. No books. No jewels. She wasn't even allowed a real window, just a metal shutter over a gaping hole. And she couldn't sneak out. The tower was too high to climb out the window. And the endless steps were so noisy that by the time she got to the bottom someone would have heard her.

(At least everyone was in great shape from clomping up and down all those winding tower stairs. In the future, an enterprising person would invent winding escalators. And then, when people were out of shape

from no more exercise, she would invent a workout program to mimic walking up stairs and sell that, too.
Eventually she would become so rich she'd buy the entire
kingdom and make it into a mall. But that's a terrible
story. Let's go back to Cinderella.)

So passed day after day. Sometimes Cinderella's stepmother was gone, but the stepsisters were always there,
watching. They made sure she worked herself to the
bone. They complained that their singed hair wasn't
growing back fast enough. They took away anything
fun. She had no time to herself. No possessions of her
own. No sparks. No joy. Poor Cinderella! Will things
ever change?

Of course they will. Otherwise this story would be
even worse than the one about escalators and malls.

On this day, as Cinderella was in the pantry organiz-
ing grains of salt by size, an official knock sounded at
the front door. Cinderella was not allowed outside without supervision. All the doors were triple-locked, and her
stepmother held the keys. But Cinderella listened at the
pantry door with interest as her stepmother spoke in low
tones, arguing.

"Of course we won't attend. It's absurd," she said.

A man answered, "It's royal orders. Every girl in the kingdom has to come to the ball."

"Why?"

"So the prince can choose a wife."

The stepmother snorted. "Why doesn't he do it the old-fashioned way?" (This was back before dating on the Internet. It used to be if you wanted to find a wife, you put an ad on the back of the community messenger pigeon. As it delivered notes, everyone saw what you had to offer. "Good hair, decent teeth, all ten fingers and nearly all ten toes. Employed cleaning pigpens. Looking for a wife with no sense of smell." If someone liked what you had to offer and met your requirements, a meeting would be arranged.)

The man sounded annoyed. "I don't know why they're doing it this way, lady! I only started working for the castle today. I'm actually a pigpen cleaner."

"Yes, I had guessed. How is your wife search going?"

"Not many girls with no sense of smell these days. Everyone has noses."

The stepmother clicked her tongue sympathetically. "Keep looking. You'll find someone."

"Thanks. Hey, I don't suppose you smell very good . . ."

"You mean to ask if I smell *well*, which I do. *And* I smell good, thank you very much!" She slammed the door. "Honestly, the rudeness of poor grammar. Girls!" she called out. "Come here."

Cinderella was there in a heartbeat, her own heart fluttering like a candle flame. Her stepsisters took longer. She thought she would die of suspense before they got there.

"What is it?" the big-headed-small-faced one asked.

"Yes, what?" the other one asked. She had a small head and a big face. If only they could trade!

"It appears we have to go to a ball. The prince needs a wife."

"The prince?" Big-head-small-face shrieked.

"A ball?" Small-head-big-face demanded.

They looked expectantly at Cinderella. Small-head-big-face elbowed her. "A wife?" Cinderella asked, because it was the only noun left that hadn't been turned into a question.

"I hear they call him Prince Charming!" Big-head-small-face said.

"I hear no one ever sees him because he's so handsome it makes women faint!" Small-head-big-face said.

"I hear wind chimes!" Cinderella said, because she did. And because she never left the house, so she never heard rumors.

"Don't get your hopes up," the stepmother said, frowning. "Something about this smells bad." She lifted the invitation, then grimaced. "Oh, no, that's left over from the pigpen cleaner who dropped it off. Well, the ball's tomorrow. So you have until then to find something to wear."

The stepsisters shrieked in joy, scrambling away. Cinderella turned to join them.

"Not so fast," the stepmother said. "You still have to finish all your work."

"But—"

"No exceptions. Back to work."

Cinderella's tears mingled with the salt, dissolving it and messing up her sorting. But she knew she would go to the ball. She had to. And she knew that she would win the heart of the prince. He would see her spark, and he would rescue her from this cold life of ashes. After all, she was the only character in this story with a name. Surely that made her more important than anyone else?

The next night, the stepsisters swept down the stairs. The stepmother looked on with silent approval. She nodded tightly. "That will do. Though why anyone would want to marry a prince, I don't know. And kings are even worse." She sighed, stroking her ring finger. On it she wore seven wedding rings. It was heavy, and they were stacked so high she couldn't bend that finger anymore. Marriage was not easy.

Cinderella had worked all day and all night. She had cleaned the cleaning supplies—scrubbing the scrubbers, polishing the polishers, and wiping the wipers, until even the memory of dirt was gone.

But she had been busy, too. Her clothes were ragged, every hem singed. Most of her skirts had small holes burned in them. But she had managed to take everything apart and make it into something new.

This is the scene where the girl shows up triumphant, having created beauty out of all the ugliness. But . . . Cinderella isn't that girl. Because instead of getting rid of the singed and burned parts, she had saved those. Her dress was a patchwork of charred fabric. She even smelled like cinders and ashes. She had used the remains of the coal in the fireplace to line her eyes and rouge her cheeks.

Her hair was piled on top of her head in swirls like smoke.

Her one concession to normal beauty was a pair of teardrop crystal earrings. The prisms winked when they caught the light. They were her last gift from her father, the only thing she had managed to hide from her step-mother all these years. She loved the way they twinkled. The way they concentrated light to a single bright, hot point. The things she knew she could do with that bright, hot point of light . . .

"Where did you get those?" Her stepmother stomped up the steps.

Cinderella put her hands over her ears. "They're mine!"

"I should have known better. You can't be allowed out. This is for your own good. Girls, grab her arms."

Cinderella cried and struggled, but it was no use. Big-head-small-face and Small-head-big-face held her while her cruel, wicked stepmother stole the earrings. Then they pushed her into the kitchen and locked the door behind her. She pounded and cried, but it was too late. They were going to the ball without her. And her last treasure was gone.

She crawled out through the cat door. Her step-mother didn't know she was little enough to fit through it, but the cat that used to live there had been very, very large. Out in the garden it was dark and cold. Sobbing and sniffling, she found two rocks and started hitting them against each other. But her heart wasn't in it.

Her spark had finally been smothered.

This is too sad. Poor Cinderella! If only there were a fairy godmother to conveniently show up and fix things. Wouldn't that be wonderful?

Oh well.

THE END

Ha ha, just kidding! Of course there's a fairy godmother. Cinderella was so busy crying that it took her a minute to notice a light glowing around her.

She looked up, surprised. "Fire?" she asked excitedly. But it wasn't a fire—it was a fairy!

Everyone knows there are three things fairies cannot resist:

1. Chubby babies with toes like little perfect bubbles. Sometimes the babies get wonderful gifts. Sometimes they get curses, though. That's why mothers always put socks on babies—best to play it safe.

2. Teeth. (What do fairies do with the teeth? That is a story for another day. A much creepier, blood-tinged day, in a dark cave lined with the teeth of generations of children, where a fairy lurks in the corner, muttering to herself as she pets your precious molars and plots how to get all the rest of them.) (Ha ha, whoops, just kidding, there's nothing creepy about a fairy sneaking into your room in the

middle of the night and taking teeth! Nothing creepy at all. Nope. Carry on!)

3. Beautiful girls crying because they have been cruelly wronged.

Cinderella fit in the last category, fortunately. I'm glad I don't have to write about the tooth fairy. She's almost as creepy as Snow White.

"Dear child," the fairy godmother said, kneeling down. "What's wrong?"

Cinderella, who never left the house and therefore didn't know you should never talk to strangers— especially glowing strangers who appear magically in your backyard—threw herself forward, hugging the fairy. "Oh, it's too awful! I was supposed to go to the ball, but they wouldn't let me!"

"Well, now," said the fairy godmother. She patted Cinderella's sleeve, then coughed at the puff of ash that drifted up. "I—" She coughed again, then cleared her throat. "I can fix that. Now, what to do about your dress?"

"Isn't it lovely?" Cinderella said, standing and twirling.

"Well, it's . . . something. But wouldn't you like a new one?"

"Oh, no. It's perfect."

The fairy godmother frowned. "I could fix it up a bit. What's your favorite color?"

"Smoke gray and flame orange!"

That was not what the fairy godmother usually got requests for. It was usually spun-sugar pink, or summer-sky blue, and she was especially good at dresses the color of dreams about unicorns. (The king would have loved that one, alas!) But she was up for the challenge. She lifted her hands and concentrated. Around Cinderella rose a skirt in brilliant yellows and oranges. The top of the dress was a shimmery gray, the fabric so light it moved like smoke.

The fairy godmother nodded. "I guess that will do. And your hair?"

Cinderella touched her hair, beaming. "Can we make it look like it's on fire?"

"O-okay?" Frowning, the fairy godmother filled the swirls of Cinderella's hair with deep red sparkles. (In later years, when her services were out of fashion, the fairy godmother would be employed in a glitter factory. She excelled at glitter.)

"And what about shoes? I can make you some nice, sensible—"

"Glass!" Cinderella shouted, a crazed gleam lighting her eyes.

"Glass?"

"Glass! Like a magnifying glass. The type you can use to light things on—" Cinderella took a deep breath, then smiled sweetly. "I mean, wouldn't glass shoes be pretty?"

This girl was certainly not what the fairy godmother had expected. She'd tell this story for years to come when getting lunch with her other fairy friends. (Not the tooth fairy—even the fairy godmother was creeped out by her.) Concentrating, she pointed her wand. Two glass slippers appeared on Cinderella's feet.

"They're perfect!" Cinderella said, spinning and laughing. "Oh, it's all perfect. How can I ever thank you?"

"By going to the ball and having the best night of your life! But you need to remember, at the strike of midnight, everything will—" The fairy godmother stopped. Cinderella was already sprinting down the road away from her. How the girl managed to run so fast in such impractical footwear, the fairy godmother had no idea. She herself could barely stand heels, and she *flew* everywhere!

"Oh well," she said. Shrugging, she poofed away. She had other stories to be in, but none of them are ours. Good-bye, Fairy Godmother! Please don't tell the tooth fairy we say hello.

Meanwhile, at the ball, the king and queen surveyed the scene in front of them miserably. The ballroom was filled to bursting with girls. The youngest was maybe twelve, or a very short fourteen. The oldest was as old as your grandma. (Wait—*is* that your grandma? I can't blame her. It's a shot at marrying a prince! Good for her.)

"I didn't realize rugs were in style," Small-head-big-face said, eyeing her own beautiful gown sadly. The queen was draped in several rugs, and the king wore dirty towels. "Or was this a costume ball and no one told us?" Everyone else had noticed, too. A few of the more fashion-forward girls had stolen rugs from other parts of the castle and thrown them over their glamorous dresses.

"Maybe they just don't know how to dress themselves." The stepmother looked around, distracted. There were no servants at all. Had something happened here?

The walls were lined with buckets of water. Everyone remarked on what a clever idea it was—like fountains inside! Only less fountainy and more . . . buckety. But since it was in a castle, they assumed it was the height of sophistication.

"It's time to release the prince," the king announced. Everyone turned and looked at him, blinking in confusion. He grimaced and tried to smile. "I mean, it's time to introduce the prince."

The queen's hands trembled as she pulled out a set of keys. Everyone watched, humming with anticipation as the queen unlocked the door. And unlocked it. And unlocked it. My, that is a lot of locks for one door!

"He must be so handsome they're afraid of kidnappers!" Small-head-big-face whispered.

"He must be so charming, they know we'd storm the castle if we could get to him," Big-head-small-face answered.

The stepmother, who knew a thing or two about why doors are locked, narrowed her eyes. Perhaps she should have accepted the king's request for her stepmotherhood, after all.

(Oh, Stepmother. If only you knew.)

Finally, after sliding one last dead bolt free, the door was ready to open. The king stood nearby with a bucket of water in his hands. Everyone held their breath as the queen opened the door to reveal . . .

SPLASH! The king threw the bucket of water, thoroughly soaking the young man before he could even walk into the ballroom. The prince's shoulders sagged and he dropped something that had been in his hand. Shaking water from his hair, the prince entered to a smattering of polite applause.

He was neither so handsome you would want to kidnap him, nor so charming you would storm a castle just to be in his presence. He looked like a guy. A wet guy. But he had a nice smile, and cute dimples, and his hair was curling now that it was wet. His eyebrows were even starting to grow back in.

Half the girls in the ballroom nodded. Good enough for them, if he came with a castle! A few slipped out, having expected more. (Oh, darn, your grandma left. I guess she's picky when it comes to princes. Better luck next time!)

Small-head-big-face and Big-head-small-face (this is confusing, I really should have asked the stepmother what their names are) were more than happy to give him a chance. They both stepped forward, smiling, but he looked right past them. No one seemed to be able to catch his eye as he strode through the ballroom, right for the fireplace. It had been bricked completely shut.

He looked disappointed. But then, from across the ballroom, he saw *her*.

She was on fire, and so was his heart.

It took him a moment to realize the girl was not actually on fire; she was simply wearing a very odd dress. A mesmerizingly beautiful dress. As he watched, she slipped out a side door. She was carrying a large stack of books. (Oh, Cinderella! She came to a ball and only wanted books!)

"Wait!" he called. He pushed through the crowds, stepping on feet and dodging attempts to talk to him.

"Prince Charming!" "Prince Charming!" "Prince— ow, you stepped on my foot!" The girls at the ball were surrounding him and he couldn't get through fast enough. Finally, with one last elbow to one last pretty nose, the crowd parted and he was out the door. He looked left and right. There was no sign of her.

But in front of him, deep in the gardens, a golden glow grew.

He ran toward it. Bushes caught on his sleeves. Branches scratched him, but he didn't care. Finally he found the source of the glow.

The girl was crouched in front of a pile of books, their pages torn free. She blew tenderly, cupping her hands around the tiny flame to protect it from the wind. (Wait a second—she's BURNING the books? What a horrible girl! I hate her! Quick, make sure she isn't burning this one, because we still have a lot of ground to cover before the end.)

"Hello," the prince said.

Cinderella squeaked in fear. Then she jumped up and stood in front of the fire to try to hide it.

"Prince Charming!" she said.

"Actually." He smiled and scooted her to the side. Then he pulled out a small bottle hidden in his pocket and poured it on the flames. They leaped higher, crackling intensely. He leaned so close that his eyebrows once again burned off. "It's Prince *Char*ring. And you are?"

"Cinderella." She turned and watched the flames as they greedily jumped to a nearby bush. She sighed in contentment.

"You don't like snakes, do you?" he asked, suddenly sounding nervous.

"They don't burn very easily, so no."

He slipped his hand into hers. "You smell like ashes," he said, leaning over and breathing deeply.

She rested her head on his shoulder. "You smell like gasoline."

It was very romantic. If you are obsessed with fires. Which I hope you are not, because that is a terrible hobby.

As the clock struck midnight, a familiar scene unfurled. Cinderella ran down the steps of the palace, losing a single glass slipper. The prince was close behind.

And the king and queen were close behind him.

And everyone else was close behind them, screaming. The now-empty castle erupted in flames.

Hmm. This is not quite how I imagined it. I don't think it's what the fairy godmother had in mind, either. Maybe the stepmother had a good reason for keeping Cinderella very, very busy at home and always locking her up?

Prince Charring caught up to Cinderella. They stood with the crowd, watching as his tower was engulfed in fire. (I'm so glad your grandmother got out of there safely!)

"At least we don't need servants to staff the castle now," the queen said.

"And we found him a wife," the king said. The queen shrugged. At this point everyone could have broken into song and she wouldn't even have had the energy to banish them.

The stepmother searched desperately through the crowds, but it was too late. There was no way she could force Cinderella to go back home now. The stepmother had failed, yet again. She shook her head. Then she made sure Big-head-small-face and Small-head-big-face were merely singed and not actively on fire. After several years with Ella, they were used to it.

Prince Charring and Cinderella looked lovely, backlit by the raging fire. They had never been so happy as they leaned in for a kiss. Theirs was a love that would burn forever.

Meanwhile, at their wedding . . .

Ring around the rosies,
Pocket full of posies,
Ashes, ashes, the castle burned down!

Ring around her finger,
Cinderella's a singer!
Ashes, ashes, the king threw his crown.

Ring around a fire,
The flames are growing higher,
Ashes, ashes, better warn the town.

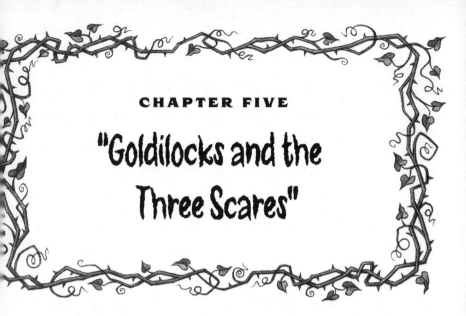

CHAPTER FIVE

"Goldilocks and the Three Scares"

Do you remember that time you were wandering around the woods by yourself and you saw a house, so you were like, "Hey! I should go in and eat their food, sit in their chairs, maybe break some stuff, and then go to sleep in their beds"?

Oh, you don't remember that time?

GOOD. Because none of that is acceptable behavior, which you are obviously smart enough to know. What kind of kid would do something like that? One without parents or responsible guardians. Unfortunately, Rapunzel and Snow White and Cinderella and Jack's stepmother couldn't be everywhere, much as she tried. Some things slipped through the cracks while she was (literally) putting out fires. One such thing the step-mother had missed is the subject of our next story. Her name is Goldilocks, and she has not learned any of the lessons about proper behavior that you have. I suspect it will get her into trouble. Let's go watch!

Goldilocks skipped through the woods, humming happily. Her locks of hair bounced in cascades of golden ringlets around her. You might think, "Ah ha! No wonder her name is Goldilocks!" She's glad you think that.

As she skipped, Goldilocks kept her eyes fixed on the forest path. Not because she was afraid of tripping—she was very coordinated—but because there were strange tracks there. Not the snake tracks she sometimes saw. These were different. Like someone had forgotten how to walk. Like they were shambling, feet dragging slowly. Here and there, scraps of red cloth had caught on branches. They decorated the path like streaks of . . .

Well, not blood! Blood would be scary and gross. Like streaks of a bright red thing that wasn't blood!

Up ahead, she saw a house, shaded and half-hidden among the looming trees. (Is it Red Riding Hood's grandmother's house? No! I wouldn't do that to you. We don't want to go in there again.) Goldilocks looked up and down the path, but the forest was silent. Eerily silent. You might even say dead silent.

Still humming, Goldilocks climbed the steps to the front door. There were deep scratch marks gouged into the wood. Shards of shattered glass crunched under her feet. A window to her left had been broken, and a sad blue curtain waved mournfully from inside, caught on the wind. Goldilocks, you really shouldn't be here!

But she didn't listen to us. The door was locked, so she pulled a small bag out of her dress pocket. Inside, gleaming as golden as her hair, were several lock picks. She crouched in front of the door and carefully worked on the lock.

It's almost like she's not some silly, stupid kid skipping aimlessly through the woods. Goldilocks looked up and winked, holding a finger in front of her lips like she was trying to shush me. The door swung open. Goldilocks went inside.

The first room was a kitchen. It was a cheerful yellow, like fresh butter. A bunch of hydrangeas in a clumsily painted vase sat on the table next to three bowls of porridge. Pease porridge, it looked like. (Oh no.) The first bowl steamed. "This porridge is too hot!" Goldilocks exclaimed, looking warily around. If it was still hot, it couldn't be that old. Goldilocks certainly notices a lot of details!

She put a finger on the side of the second bowl. "This porridge is too cold." If it was still cold, it couldn't have been out for that long, either. Goldilocks knew that hot porridge and cold porridge both turn into room temperature porridge eventually. She paused and listened, but the house was silent. Except there—a small groan. Well, this was an old house. It could have been simply the house settling on its foundation, or the wind, or some ghastly fate awaiting this poor, innocent girl.

Probably just the wind, though.

Goldilocks leaned over the third bowl. She picked up the spoon next to it and dipped it into the porridge. "But this one is just . . ." Her nose wrinkled. "Just the most awful thing I have ever smelled in my life." Gagging, she dropped the spoon. The porridge spilled out. There was another splatter on the table, as if someone had already done the exact same thing.

Goldilocks left the kitchen. The next room was a family room. Fishing magazines open to centerfold spreads of salmon were left out on a coffee table. There was a well-loved picture book called *The Kidenstain Kids*. A "Three Is a Magic Number" cross-stitch was lying half-finished on the floor. There were also three chairs.

The first was a humongous chair, with stiff, dark hairs that looked like fur all over the wood. "This chair is too hard," she said.

The second chair was decorated with a floral pattern. The cushion was worn thin, sinking so low it almost touched the floor. Whoever regularly sat in this chair was much, much larger than Goldilocks. And, judging by the way the armrests were shredded, had much sharper claws. I mean, fingernails. "This chair is too soft," Goldilocks said.

She turned to the third chair in the room. It was made of solid wood. Small, as if for a child, but sturdy. "This chair is . . ." I see where this is going. Goldilocks, you shouldn't break into strange houses and sit in their chairs!

She glared, then leaned over and picked up a piece of wooden chair leg, shaking it up at me. "This chair is just smashed to pieces." She hefted the splintered chair leg, wondering what could have broken such a well-made chair.

Goldilocks yawned. She hadn't slept well in so long. Those strange tracks kept her up at night. So much to do. Down the hall she could see a bedroom. The thought of a nice, warm, safe bed called to her. Keeping the chair leg in her hand, she walked silently into the bedroom.

The wall was covered with children's art. But the kid wasn't a very good artist! All the people had ears on top of their heads and long noses more like snouts. Their hands were clumsily painted to look like massive paws.

Goldilocks considered them thoughtfully, feeling for whether the paint was dry. *I'm getting so nervous. I wish she'd just hurry up.*

With an exasperated huff, she looked at the rest of the long room. There were three beds. The first bed had the mattress ripped clean off. It had been thrown against the wall, where it drooped brokenly. Goldilocks put a hand on the wooden slats of the bed frame. "This bed is too hard," she said.

The second bed was a feather mattress. Goldilocks knew this because feathers were still floating lazily in the air, freed from the mattress by several deep gouges that had been clawed in it. One feather brushed her nose and she sneezed. "This bed is too soft."

The third bed was smaller than the first two, a perfect size for a large child or perhaps a small bear. (I always measure my furniture in terms of bear sizes. For example, the couch I am sitting on is medium bear–size. My bed is large bear–size. My bathroom is no bear–size, because bears don't use indoor plumbing, except in horrible toilet paper commercials.)

Though the quilts on this bed had been ripped up, there were a lot of them.

"This bed is just right," Goldilocks declared, and she crawled under the blankets, covering herself up.

Wake up, Goldilocks! I whisper desperately. *You* really *shouldn't sleep here.* But she doesn't move. If you didn't know she was there, you wouldn't ever guess. She's so still. So silent.

Not silent was the front door as it slowly creaked open. Three shapes—one hulking, one slightly less hulking, and one that would be hulking in the future but for now was more cuddly-adorable—came into the kitchen.

I know how this part goes! First, Papa Bear will say, "Someone has been eating my porridge."

Papa Bear stumbled into the table, knocking it over. The three bowls of porridge crashed to the ground. "Braaaaaiiiiins," he growled.

Oh. That is—well, that is not what I thought he would say. But look! Now they are going into the room with the chairs. "Someone has been sitting in my chair!" is the line you are looking for, Mama Bear.

Mama Bear dragged her feet across the floor, powerful arms held out in front of her as she passed her chair without even noticing it. "Braaaaaaiiiiiiins," she growled.

This isn't going at all how I expected. I'm confused, and even more worried for poor little Goldilocks than I was before. She has no idea what's coming!

The three bears groaned and shambled slowly toward the bedroom. Papa Bear dragged his long claws along the end of his bed. Someone hasn't been sleeping in his bed!

Mama Bear snuffed slowly, her red eyes unblinking. Someone hasn't been sleeping in her bed, either!

Baby Bear stopped in front of his bed. His adorable little bear snout under his genuinely terrifying red eyes sniffed and sniffed. "Braaaaaaaiiiiiiiiins?" he groaned. Someone had been sleeping in his bed, and there she was!

Goldilocks jumped up, whacking Baby Bear across his sensitive nose with her chair leg club. "Come and get me, zombears!" she screamed. Ducking under Mama Bear's powerful paw as it swiped through the air, Goldilocks rolled. She dove between Papa Bear's legs. His jaws snapped around where her head had been mere seconds before.

She threw the chair leg through the nearest window,

shattering it. Then she jumped out, catching a tree branch and hanging in the air. She turned around, facing the window. The three bears were still inside, groaning for brains, thick saliva matting their fur.

"I've got your brains right here!" Goldilocks shouted. (No, sweet little girl, run! Run for your life!)

The bears roared. First, Papa Bear climbed out the window. But Goldilocks was too high, and he fell down. Right through a screen of branches and into a cage.

Next, Mama Bear climbed out the window. But Goldilocks was too high, and Mama Bear fell down into the cage.

Finally, Baby Bear climbed out the window. He stood on the sill and reached for Goldilocks, his sharp claws catching on her boots. She wrapped her feet around his neck and tugged back, pulling him out the window and straight down into the trap.

She dropped down and slammed the lid shut, pulling a set of golden locks out of her bag.

The first lock was too big.

The second lock was too small.

But the third lock was just right.

Oh! I get it! GOLDILOCKS.

Goldilocks sighed, flipping her hair back and glaring up at me. "Do you mind?" she asked. "I'm kind of trying to hunt zombies here, and your commentary isn't exactly helping."

Right. Sorry. We'll leave her to her work, then, and move right along to another part of the forest. Preferably one with fewer zombears.

Meanwhile,
Red Riding Hood . . .

What are little boys made of?
Snips and snails and puppy dog tails,
That's what little boys are made of!

What are little girls made of?
Brains and wails and people entrails,
That's what little girls are made of!

CHAPTER SIX

"Jack the Beanstalker"

When Jack finally found his stepmother, she smelled like fire and exhaustion. They met on the edge of a town. In the distance, smoke curled lazily from the ruins of the castle. His stepmother held a gleaming red apple.

"Can I have that?" Jack asked.

"No!" She slapped his hand away. "I thought you were with Jill and her family!"

"Didn't work out," Jack muttered. He was still bitter about being pushed into the well. Which is a perfectly reasonable reaction to being pushed into a well.

"Did you find a job in a castle, then?"

"Didn't work out." This time Jack had the decency to blush, because that one had been entirely his fault. Think of how much trouble could have been avoided if Jack had been willing to eat vegetables! Then he would have known that *pea* and *pee* are very different things. Peas really aren't so bad, you know. Unless you stick them up your nose as a joke to make your parents laugh, and then one gets stuck, and you have to go to the doctor and have it removed with a long, terrifying tool, and you can't eat peas for years afterward because you were so traumatized. I'm, umm, not speaking from personal experience or anything. Seriously: DON'T STICK PEAS UP YOUR NOSE. And let's get back to Jack.

"Can't I come live with you again?" Jack asked.

His stepmother pursed her lips. That doesn't mean she turned her lips into a purse, though that would be very impressive. It means she pushed them tightly together in a sign that Jack was not going to get what he hoped for. "Sweetheart, I'm sorry. I have too many other things going on right now. I still haven't heard back from that idiot huntsman." She looked with worry at the apple, then tucked it into her cloak. "Cinderella and her husband are liable to burn down the whole kingdom. I haven't seen Rapunzel in weeks. I think her fair Herr might have eaten her."

Jack did not understand how anyone could be eaten

by her own fair hair! We should introduce him to the prince so they can teach each other some spelling.

But his stepmother was still talking. "And that's to say nothing of all the stepsisters I'm in charge of. No, Jack, what you need is another job."

Jack didn't think that was fair. He wasn't very old. But back then they didn't have any nice child labor laws. If you said, "But I'm a kid!" they'd agree that was a very useful thing to be. They'd then send you up a chimney or down a mine, like a pea in a nose.

"Here," his stepmother said, handing him the reins to a cow. (Did I mention she had a cow with her? I must have forgotten in my distraction over remembering that horrible tool the doctor had to use to get that pea out.) "I was going to train this cow to jump over the moon, but I guess I don't ever get the time to do what *I* want to. You'll have to lead the cow to good pastures and water, and milk her three times a day. You can sell the milk in markets, or make it into butter or cheese and sell that."

Jack wrinkled his nose. The cow didn't smell very good. (But it did smell very well, which meant it was yet another female that wouldn't marry the pigpen cleaner. Poor guy.) And all that leading the cow around, milking her, and making butter seemed like an awful lot of work. "Isn't there something else I can do, instead? Can I sell the cow for quick cash?"

"You've got to stop thinking short-term, Jack. That cow will provide a solid living, which is worth more than a one-time bag full of coins." She sighed, regretfully looking up at the moon, barely visible in the blue sky. "Next time," she whispered. "Then all I need is a cat and a fiddle . . ."

"What?" Jack asked.

"Nothing! You should get to work."

Kicking moodily at the dirt, Jack tugged on the reins. And tugged. And tugged. It turns out cows are very large, and also are not super fond of being dragged around by grouchy little boys. I can't really blame her for that. Finally, mooing reproachfully, the cow followed him.

Jack took a path through the forest, looking for a promising meadow. But he didn't see anything that looked comfortable enough to nap in. He was about to turn around and head back toward civilization when he stopped in amazement.

Rising up from the ground in an impassable wall was a tangle of vines. The wall stretched as far as he could see in either direction. There was no way around it, and no way through it.

Well, almost no way through it. Light shone from a narrow gap. Behind it, he could see a man kneeling on the ground. He was dressed like a gardener. Which is less interesting than being dressed like a garden, but also less likely to have thorns in your underpants. Underplants? See, this is why no one dresses like a garden.

"Hey!" Jack said.

The man looked up, startled. "What are you doing here?"

"What is *this* doing here?" Jack pointed at the plant wall.

The gardener leaned back, wiping sweat from his forehead. "Leftover from an enchanted castle. Our princess bought it and hired me. Your kingdom is grounded."

"We're—what?"

"She put you all in time-out."

Jack frowned, until he remembered that horrible princess. The last one that had visited the castle. He supposed this was, in a way, his fault. If only he had known the queen meant a pea rather than a pee!

The gardener was leaning through the hole.

"That's a very nice cow you have. It looks like she smells great."

"Do you mean she smells good, or she smells well? It's a very confusing distinction."

"I've been looking for a cow. I want to get out of the magic plant wall business, become a sculptor instead."

"How would a cow help with that?" Jack asked.

"I want to be a butter sculptor. People will come from far and wide to see the wonders I could make out of creamy white butter! I'll be the most famous butter sculptor in the world!"

"There probably isn't a lot of competition for that title," Jack said, trying not to laugh. But Jack was wrong. The art of butter sculpting has a long and illustrious history. Most of the famous sculptures you know are actually stone replicas of far more amazing butter sculptures. Even the Leaning Tower of Pisa was modeled after a glorious butter tower. (That's why it's leaning—the butter had started melting, because butter isn't known for its structural integrity. But the architect who was copying the sculpture didn't realize it wasn't supposed to be that way.) This gardener would go on to a streak of second-place finishes in local butter sculpting contests. The cow, on the other hand, would be renowned among all her kind for her excellent sense of smell. Cows know the difference between smelling good and smelling well, and they appreciate it.

"Can I buy the cow?" the gardener asked.

Jack remembered what his stepmother had said. "It's worth more than a bag of coins."

"Of course it is! I would never give you money for the cow. I have these instead." He stuck his hand through the hole in the vines, holding out three small beans. Please remember that our friend Jack is utterly clueless when it comes to any sort of vegetable. And while beans are actually legumes, not vegetables, Jack didn't know that, either.

The gardener whispered in his most dramatic voice, "These are *magic* beans."

"Magic?" Jack asked. Magic was more valuable than money! Jack had had money before, but he'd never had magic.

"Magic!" the gardener repeated.

Just then the cow passed a tremendous amount of gas. It did not smell good, and Jack smelled well, so he got the full power of the cow-pow. "Take it!" he said, grabbing the beans and passing the reins (but not reigns or rains) to the gardener.

After a great struggle, the gardener finally managed to coax the cow through the small gap in the vines. "Thanks, kid!" he said. Then he dropped a seed smaller than the beans into the gap. Plants immediately grew, filling it in. Jack was staring at a now totally impassable wall of green.

For a moment, he wondered if he had made a mistake. But beans were light and much easier to drag around a forest than the cow had been. He skipped along, thinking how proud his stepmother would be when he showed her that he had traded a plain old cow for *magic*.

You and I, of course, know better than Jack. Obviously you should never trade something real for something "magic." Until the magic has been clearly demonstrated, the mechanics of how everything works thoroughly explained, *and* you've been given a detailed receipt with a return policy. After that, by all means, trade your phone for that carpet or lamp or handful of beans! Your parents will be so pleased.

But all that happy-forest skipping had made Jack tired. He found a small meadow nestled into the trees. It wasn't good for a cow, but it was perfect for a Jack. Yawning, he curled up with the beans in his fist and fell asleep.

Here are two things you need to know about Jack's sleeping habits:

1. He's a drooler. An epic drooler. You could wring out his pillowcase in the morning and fill several buckets with spit. Why you would want buckets of spit, I don't know, but I'm not here to judge your hobbies. At least you don't light things on fire.

2. He's a wriggler. Some people sleep as still as stone and as silent as death. Those people are really terrifying, and you should always poke them to wake them up and make sure they're still breathing. It's their own fault for being creepy. Some people move around a little, snoring and snuffling and otherwise politely letting you know they're still alive. And some people, like Jack, sleep like they are being electrocuted.

So, over the course of his nap, the beans were flung from his hand. They landed near his face, where the drool was already puddling. The beans sucked up the spit, because beans are stupid and do not understand that water is good but spit is *disgusting*. And then they began to grow.

And grow.

And grow.

AND GROW SO HIGH

that the top of the thick, twisting stalk disappeared into the clouds above.

Jack awoke, shivering. He was cold because (a) he was sleeping in a puddle of his own drool and (b) because the stalk had grown so thick that he was now in the shade instead of the sun.

"Oh, pee porridge," Jack cursed with a frown. His beans had not turned out how he had expected. And with no receipt, he couldn't return them. (It might not have mattered anyway, because the gardener could have claimed the beans were not returned in the same condition they were given and refused a refund. You should always get the return policy in writing and read the small print.)

He had no money, no beans, and no cow. He couldn't very well go back to his stepmother like this. And he couldn't leave the kingdom, not with that wall of vines all around it. There was no castle to go to for work anymore, even if they would have taken him again (they wouldn't have). He'd never go back to Jill with her stupid red cloak and her even stupider habit of pushing people into wells.

He looked up.

UP AND UP AND UP

to where the stalk pierced the clouds. He had always wondered what it would be like to sleep on a cloud. He imagined it would be light and fluffy, warm and wonderful. Jack could never pass up an opportunity for a nap, even when he had just woken up from one. So he began to climb.

It's a very long climb, so while he's climbing, let's take a look around the kingdom. There, a small fire burning. Hi, Cinderella! Hi, Prince Charring! They're just the cutest couple, aren't they?

There, a small girl with golden curls carefully following tracks in the forest. Goldilocks doesn't want us spooking her prey, though, so we'll move on.

There, the tail end of a very long, slithery body slipping into some undergrowth. Let's not stay here.

There, a ragged red hood over ragged red eyes. "Brains?" Red Riding Hood says, looking up at us. Moving right along again, much faster!

There, a big bag that was supposed to be left in the middle of a sunny meadow. What is it doing in the depths of the darkest part of the forest? And why is the huntsman sleeping so quiet and still with two red marks on the side of his neck? Maybe I should—

Oh, look! Jack made it to the top. The clouds stretched out all around him. Jack took a deep breath, then jumped from the stalk toward the clouds.

Jack laughed, bouncing up and down. The clouds were springy beneath him, like walking on a giant trampoline made of cotton candy. Jack bent down and scooped up a handful of cloud, licking it. It even tasted like cotton candy! I guess no one ever told Jack that clouds are just cold water vapor. Science ruins everything for us, doesn't it?

But, not knowing science, Jack didn't have to obey its rules. He flipped and jumped and bounced across the clouds. I'm so jealous of him, I'd like to pour a big bowl of pease porridge on his head. But he wouldn't stay still long enough for us to do that.

He saw a house nearby. He ran toward it . . . and then ran some more and then some more. He realized the house hadn't been close—it was so enormously huge and hugely enormous that he thought it was a normal-size house close by, rather than a giant-size house far away.

By the time Jack got to it, he was exhausted. Cloud bouncing is fun at first, but it's actually an even more strenuous workout than all those tower stairs. (If Jack had any sense, he would have created an exercise program of cloud bouncing and been set for life. But then again, Jack wasn't good at thinking long-term.)

All he could think of was getting something to eat and finding somewhere to take a nap. (I have to agree with Jack for once. Those are my own top priorities at any given time.) He tried the door, but the handle was several Jacks high, and he was the only Jack there. Looking around, he found a giant-size mouse hole in the foundation. But a giant-size mouse hole also doubles as a normal-size boy hole. Jack crawled into it.

Halfway through the long, dark hole, Jack had a horrible thought: If the house was giant-size, and the mice were giant-size . . . what size would spiders be? With a scream (I don't know if it was him screaming or you, but I don't blame anyone), he threw himself out of the hole and into a kitchen. The fireplace alone was bigger than any house Jack had lived in. Cinderella and Prince Charring would have cried with joy at seeing it. The table was two stories high. A broom the size of a sequoia tree leaned in the corner.

Jack set off to explore.

Maybe that isn't wise, Jack. Because gigantic houses

with gigantic furniture and gigantic brooms and gigantic knives hanging on the wall don't simply appear. They exist because someone—or something—has need of such giganticness.

But Jack, as always, ignored me. He tried climbing up the table leg to see if there was any food up there, but he couldn't manage it. Far across the floor, such a great distance away he had to squint, he saw some jars and burlap bags.

His stomach rumbled the whole five minutes it took to walk there. The jars were too large to open, but he managed to tear a hole in one of the bags. Round things bigger than his head tumbled out. He was buried in an avalanche of green. By the time he worked himself free, he was covered in peas. But at least he wasn't covered in pee! And now he knew the difference.

The first thing he did was try to stick one of the peas up his nose. How many times do I have to tell you what a terrible idea that is?! Fortunately, because the pea was as big as his head, this was impossible. He nibbled on it for a bit, but dried peas aren't very yummy. So he went from bag to bag, cutting them open and nibbling on whatever fell out; mostly huge vegetables, none of which he liked. One bag was filled with bread crumbs. Jack normally loved bread, but this loaf was weirdly dry and tasted like a cemetery smells. He didn't eat much of it. Another bag had sugar crystals as big as his hands. He licked one, sitting against the bag and putting his dirty shoes up.

Let's take a moment to make a list of the ways in which Jack is not being a good houseguest.

1. He didn't wipe his feet or take off his shoes before coming in.

2. He didn't bring a gift for his host.

3. He showed up without any advance notice or even being invited.

4. He didn't know there were three meanings for the word *stalk*. One was a type of plant that grew out of the ground and, in some magical cases, straight up into the sky. The second was to harass someone and trespass on their property, causing damage both physical and

psychological. Jack really should have known this definition, since that's basically what he was doing. The third was to pursue and stealthily hunt prey. Jack will become *very* familiar with this part of the definition by the end of the book.

So any of those reasons makes him a bad houseguest, but the fourth most of all. No one likes a beanstalker.

Still unapologetic for his actions, Jack was full to bursting after eating so many things. But his stomach was rumbling again. And the rumbling was getting louder and louder. It started to sound like—singing? Why was his stomach singing? And why did his stomach have such a deep, deep voice?

The door slammed open. The noise was like an earthquake. It brought Jack to his knees. Then another earthquake—cloudquake?—struck. Then another, and another. That's when Jack saw the boots that were bigger than if you gathered up everything Jack didn't know about vegetables and put it into a sack. (It would have to be a very big sack, too.)

FEE

Jack screamed, covering his ears. He burrowed under one of the sacks, letting the weight of the contents and material dampen some of the noise. See, Jack, you should never break into strangers' homes. Unless you have golden hair and golden locks and are highly skilled at tracking and trapping zombies. But even Goldilocks would have thought twice before taking on a giant!

FIE

What could Jack do? He couldn't make a run for it! There was a football-field length between him and the mouse hole. He would never make it out before the giant saw him.

FOE

If only he had kept the cow. He missed that stupid, gassy cow. He would do anything to have her back. He would milk her, and feed her, and make butter sculptures of her. He would find her the best pastures. Maybe someday they would settle down and start a family. (Not together, of course, because while the cow was attractive for a cow, she wasn't Jack's type. But they could each find someone of their own species to marry, and his kids and her calves could grow up together, best friends, probably equally smelly.)

Now he didn't have a cow, and he probably didn't have a future, either.

FUM

Jack trembled. The items in the bag were hard, digging into his back. He wriggled around, pulling one out. It was a golden coin as big as his head. With this much gold, he could buy his cow back! He could buy all the cows in the world! He could be the Grand Cow Master, Owner of All the Cows, and he would never take them for granted again!

Or he could buy cooler things than cows. That's probably what he'd do. If he ever got out of here alive.

|

Gee, this giant sure did talk slow. Jack had had enough time now to calm down. He wasn't even panicked anymore. It was really uncomfortable, smashed here under all this gold. He wished the giant would finish whatever he was saying and then leave.

SMELL

Was the giant saying, "I smell?" Jack sniffed the air. Yes, that was accurate. Jack wriggled around until he was more comfortable. Yawning, he closed his eyes. He napped through the rest of what the giant was calling, the rumbles almost comforting. Like a big, terrifying massage.

THE BLOOD OF AN ENGLISH-MUN

Jack woke up, stretching, trying to work out some of the kinks in his neck. Sleeping under a huge sack of gold wasn't the worst place he had ever taken a nap, but it wasn't the best.

He started to wriggle out, but

BE

Oh great. The giant wasn't done yet. Jack banged his head against the gold coin in frustration.

HE

Jack couldn't take much more of this. Not only was it like having a thunderstorm in his head, it was also taking way too long. Jack was bored. And he really, really had to pee. There were no mattresses around, either. Or a toilet. He sometimes used toilets, too.

ALIVE

Honestly, Jack, you got yourself into this mess. It serves you right to have to sit here and listen to this for the next several hours. I don't feel sorry for you.

OR

Fine, no, I can't stand it anymore, either. Run for it, Jack!

BE

Certain he was about to be squashed like a pea, Jack darted out from under the sack. He raced under the table. A giant hand swooped down in slow motion. The wind from it knocked Jack flat on his back. But he scrambled away from the fingers, each as big as he was, just in time.

HE

He could see the mouse hole now, but the giant was dragging the table away! Jack wouldn't have any cover then. The sound of the table scraping against the floor was terrible. Jack ran as fast as he could.

DEAD

He didn't need to worry too much. What the giant had in size, he lacked in speed. A foot slammed down where Jack had been seconds before, easily missing him. Jack darted to one side. Then to the other. Every boot smash was an earthquake, every hand grab a hurricane. Jack was buffeted to and fro. But he was getting closer and closer to his escape!

Jack screeched to a halt. The giant crouched down in front of the wall, blocking Jack's escape! The giant put his face against the floor. He fixed one eyeball on Jack. The eyeball was half as tall as Jack, and far rounder. (Which is good—it would be weird to have an eyeball that was person-shaped. Then it would be less of an eyeball and more of an eyecylinder.)

GRIND

Jack had no other way to get out. The door was closed. The windows were two stories up. All Jack had was the huge gold coin, still clutched against his chest.

HIS

Jack debated his options. He needed this coin! But he needed to stay alive more than that. The giant's hand was coming down from above.

BONES

"Argh!" Jack shouted, throwing the coin like a Frisbee. It cut through the air, smashing against the giant's eye. The giant blinked, flinching away. Jack darted through the new opening. He was in the mouse hole! He was safe!

TO

A rush of wind pushed at his back. He tumbled through the mouse hole, not even pausing to imagine giant spiders this time. (I won't, either, or else I won't be able to sleep tonight.) The giant had his mouth to the hole and was still shouting.

MAKE

Jack somersaulted out of the hole. He hit the clouds running. In the distance was his beanstalk, his way home.

MY

At the beanstalk, gasping for breath, Jack paused. He had waited this long to get the whole message. He hated to go down without hearing the end of it. The giant would grind his bones to make what?

BREAD!

"Bread?" Jack said, flinging his arms up. "You'll grind my bones to make *bread*? That's disgusting! Who would ever want to eat bread made out of bones? It would taste like—" Jack put a hand over his mouth, horrified. He knew exactly what it would taste like, because he had eaten some.

Oh dear. Look the other way, please. You don't want to watch this next part.

Jack threw up all over those fluffy white clouds as you wisely looked across the horizon. There were a lot of houses up here, not just one. It looked like a whole cloud land, full of giants. You had better get going, Jack.

"I know, I know," he muttered, his stomach sore and empty now. He had a long climb down ahead of him. He had no gold. He had no cow. He didn't even have any magic beans anymore.

And that, my friends, is why you always ask for a receipt. And also why you don't break into giants' homes or eat food that doesn't have an ingredient label. But mostly the first one.

Meanwhile, in the forest . . .

Rock-a-bye baby,
In the treetops
Who put you up there?
Let's call the cops.
The cops are all zombies,
So is the town
You're safe up there,
We won't get you down.

CHAPTER SEVEN

"Bad Apple"

On further thought, perhaps I should have stayed and examined what, exactly, was going on with that empty sack and that unmoving huntsman. The queen had been very specific about how he was supposed to leave the sack with Snow White in the middle of a sunny meadow. But there it was, in the middle of the deepest, darkest woods. Maybe we should go back and take a look.

Nah! I'm sure everything is totally fine.

Let's go visit this old woman who lives in a shoe. All her kids smell like dirty socks, she doesn't feed them much, and she whips them before bed. It's hilarious—you're going to love it.

No? You . . . *want* to go into the deepest, darkest woods? But nothing good ever happens there!

Fine. Don't say I didn't warn you.

On this day, in the deepest, darkest part of the woods, seven dwarves were trudging home. Their cloaks were pulled tightly over their faces, and they squinted against what few dim rays of sunlight managed to fight their way through the thick cover of trees.

The forest here was old: gnarled and knotted, mossed and rotted. It smelled like decay. Even the birds singing in the tree were off-key, their tweeting more like funeral dirges than cheerful birdsong. Even though it was daytime, the cold never quite left. On the brightest summer afternoon, the air down here was damp and chill. It seemed to tug with clammy fingers. (Are you really sure you want to be here? I know a lot of other stories! We can visit them, instead!)

Snow White threw open the windows of the seven dwarves' cottage, singing her own funeral tune with all the joy her little unbeating heart could contain. Oh my! I had forgotten how beautiful she was! How sweet and good! How much I loved staring into her black, black eyes. I don't want to be anywhere else but here.

Snow White was happy. Now that she wasn't trapped in that wretched castle, she could do as she pleased! First, she had enjoyed such a nice meal with that big stupid huntsman. Then she had found seven little dwarves who simply loved her to *death*. It had been so long since anyone adored her! Her stepmother certainly hadn't. That horrible woman had never done anything to make Snow White happy. And now she had seven little friends who lived to do whatever she asked of them!

It was perfect.

For now.

Soon, though, Snow White would move on. Because she was so happy and she made the seven dwarves so happy. She needed to spread that happiness to the next village, and the next! But even that would not be enough. She would only truly be happy when every single person in the kingdom—and then the world—knew and loved her.

She licked her bloodred lips. Oh, yes. Everyone would love her. Don't you love her? Yes, you do. Look deep into those bottomless black eyes. Snow White will make everyone love her, and when they love her, they'll all be happy! Thank you, Snow White, for being so generous!

Her mesmerizing voice had called the seven dwarves back. She smiled, showing each tiny, sharp tooth. "Good afternoon," she trilled happily. "How are my favorite dwarves?"

The first dwarf took off his hood. He was ashen and pale, with dark circles under his eyes. "Actually," he said, his voice gravelly and tortured, "we're not dwarves. Remember? We're just very hirsute children." (*Hirsute* is a fun word! It means covered with excessive hair. An easy way to remember is that if you look like you are wearing a hair suit, you are very hirsute. There's nothing wrong with being hirsute. It makes you softer and warmer than everyone else. Unfortunately for these seven boys, it also made Snow White confuse them for dwarves.)

Snow White hummed, nodding. "Yes, yes, of course, my little dwarves. Now come in! It's time to eat!"

That's odd. There was nothing on the table or the stove. No delicious scents of food filled the air. Snow White tied a cloth napkin around her neck and smiled as the hirsute boys filed in one by one. Then she licked her lips again, and closed the door.

Not too far from where we left the sounds of Snow White gleefully slurping her dinner, the queen found something troubling.

This was not the queen who was currently sitting on the burned rubble heap of her former castle. *That* queen would no sooner go searching in the darkest part of the forest than she would brush her own teeth without a servant's help. Which was why she also had a serious toothache.

No, this queen was the queen who had married the king, who had been married to the queen, who had died, who had then died himself, but not before marrying this queen. (Royal marriage is complicated.) This was the queen who had sent the huntsman into the forest with Snow White. The queen who had tried to end Snow White's precious little life once Snow White became the fairest in all the land.

That queen. (She looks very familiar! She and the stepmother could be the same person. WAIT. Oh, no wonder she's so exhausted!)

She sighed as she picked up the empty sack Snow White had been in. This was not the middle of a sunny meadow. She looked around. I held my breath, waiting for her to find the huntsman where we had seen him lying motionless.

But there was nothing there. Whew! That was a relief.

"Hello," the huntsman said from behind her.

"Aaaaaugh!" I screamed.

Fortunately, the queen was more used to terrifying things than I am. She was, after all, the stepmother of Snow White among many others. She calmly turned around. The huntsman loomed in the shadows beneath a tree. His eyes seemed to shine almost red in the midst of his unnaturally pale face. Two red dots on the side of his neck matched his eyes.

"There you are," said the queen. "I take it you did not follow my instructions."

"I'm thirsty," said the huntsman. He ran his tongue along his teeth as he stared at the queen's long, graceful throat.

"Of course you are." The queen smiled. "Where is Snow White?"

"She said I'm not supposed to tell you."

"Of course not. You absolutely shouldn't tell me that she went back to the castle and is living in the village."

The huntsman frowned. "No, I'm not supposed to tell you that she's in the darkest part of the woods, living in a cottage with seven hirsute children."

"Right," the queen said. "Of course. Is there anything else you weren't supposed to do?"

The huntsman frowned, scratching his chin with his dirty fingernails. "I wasn't supposed to give you any warning before I bit you?" His face fell. "I messed it up, didn't I? She was so specific! And I don't want to disappoint her. Beautiful Snow White. Good Snow White. Sweet Snow White."

"Don't worry! We don't have to tell her. I have an idea. I'll go stand in the middle of that meadow—the sunny one you were supposed to leave her in—and you can sneak up behind me there. That way you'll be doing exactly what she told you to do."

The huntsman smiled, showing his newly pointed teeth. "Gee, you'd do that for me?"

"It's the least I can do to repay you for all your work." The queen stalked back through the trees to the meadow. She stood in the middle. The brilliant sunshine was like a blanket around her. Then, after hearing a surprised shriek and *poof* sound, the queen turned around. She lifted her skirts and stepped over the huntsman-size pile of ash on the edge of the meadow.

Out of her bag, she pulled a cloak and some makeup. She drew lines on her face and attached a false nose. She drank lemon juice so her voice was tight and scratchy. If you hadn't seen her do it, you would never have known that beneath that hooded cloak and weird makeup was the queen herself.

Leaning heavily on a long, sturdy stick, she slowly hobbled through the trees. "Apples!" she called. "Apples for sale!"

Deep in the darkest part of the forest, she found one of the poor little hirsute boys leaning against a tree. His eyes were dull, his lips pale. He was not yet fairer than she was, though. "Hello, little boy," she said.

"You don't think I'm a dwarf?" the boy asked.

"I think you grow a very fine beard for such a young child. You should be proud. Tell me, would anyone around here like to buy some fresh fruit?"

He shook his head sadly. But then his eyebrows drew low in thought. "Maybe," he whispered, "maybe if we found her the right food . . ."

"Her?" the queen asked.

"Come on!" the hirsute boy said. He scrambled ahead of her, stumbling and tripping. He had to stop and rest a lot. The queen was impatient. But she was pretending to be an old woman, so she couldn't very well tell him to go faster. Finally, they drew close to a quaint cottage. No smoke rose from the chimney.

"Don't you get cold?" the queen asked. "You should light a fire."

"Oh, no!" he squeaked. "No fires allowed!" He pushed her toward the cottage. "See if you can get her to eat something. Anything. Anything but . . ." He put a hand over the side of his neck and swallowed hard.

"Why don't you run away?" the queen asked, crouching down to look him in the eyes. For a moment, she thought he would listen to her. Then his eyes went fuzzy again, like a television switched to the wrong channel. Nothing there but static.

"I would miss her too much," he said. "Beautiful Snow White. Sweet Snow White."

"Good Snow White. I know, I know." Sighing, the queen stood up, straightening her cloak and bending her back. "A stepmother's got to do what a stepmother's got to do," she muttered. "In other words, what literally no one else is willing to."

She knocked her walking stick against the door.

The door slowly creaked open. "Yes?" Snow White said. (I should be smart like the queen and avoid looking directly into her eyes.)

The queen reached into her bag and withdrew the gleaming apple. It shone bright red. She held it out. "Apple, my dear?"

Snow White hissed, flinching away. "No! Never!"

Darn. I thought that was going to work! The queen dropped the apple back into her bag. She pulled out a banana. "Banana?" She was used to picky stepchildren.

Snow White made retching noises.

"Brussels sprout?"

"Does anyone actually like those?"

The queen shrugged, dropping it back in her bag. "It was worth a shot. Pea?"

"No, thank you, I just went to the bathroom."

Biting back a growl of frustration, the queen pulled out one final item. Her last chance. "How about . . . a *blood* orange?"

If you were looking into Snow White's eyes, you

would have seen the black there gleam with a reddish, hungry light. "Did you say blood?"

The queen smiled. "Go on, try it. They're very juicy."

Snow White snatched the blood orange away. She peeled it in a frenzy, then opened her mouth and sank her fangs into it. Her black eyes went wide before rolling back into her head. She collapsed, unmoving, unbreathing.

The queen stared down sadly. The seven hirsute children gathered around her, crying. They wiped their eyes with their beards. "She was so beautiful!" they cried.

"And so good and so sweet, yes, I know." The queen sighed.

"We should bury her!" one of the boys said.

"But then we would never get to see her again!"

"I know!" the tallest of the hirsute boys said. "I have a glass coffin."

Everyone paused. "*Why* do you have a glass coffin?" the queen asked.

"I collect them. You know, like how some people collect baseball cards, or rocks shaped like hearts. I collect glass coffins."

The queen frowned. "Well, at least your hobby isn't arson. I suppose that—" But then she heard a strange rumbling. Looking up through a break in the trees, she saw, far in the distance, a very tall stalk going straight up into the clouds. And a very tiny figure—a suspiciously Jack-shaped figure—scrambling down it.

She looked the other direction, where black smoke was billowing up into the sky. It practically spelled out Cinderella. No . . . it *actually* spelled out Cinderella. She and her husband really were quite good with fire.

The queen looked back down at Snow White. "Glass coffin, you say? Sounds good. Put her inside and take her to the middle of the sunniest meadow you can find."

The seven hirsute children nodded, sniffling and sobbing. The queen muttered, pointing back and forth between the beanstalk and the smoke. "One stepchild, two stepchild, three stepchild, four. Which rotten stepchild needs me more?" Sighing, she went off in the direction of the smoke.

The seven hirsute children slowly dragged the glass coffin toward the meadow. But it was hard work and they *were* only children, regardless of how much facial hair they had. By the time they got the coffin to the meadow, it was twilight. Everything was soft and purple and decidedly not-sunny.

"Hello!" a cheerful voice called.

The seven hirsute children stopped laying flowers on Snow White's coffin. Approaching them was a nice-looking young man on top of a horse with no eyebrows. The young man, not the horse. The horse didn't have eyebrows because she was a horse. The young man didn't have eyebrows because he didn't understand basic fire safety. A girl rode with her arms snug around his waist. They were both covered in soot and ashes and smelled like smoke.

"What happened here?" he asked, climbing off the horse and peering into the coffin. "She's beautiful!"

"And sweet and good," the hirsute children said, sobbing. One of them looked up hopefully. "Would you like to kiss her?"

"I—uh, wow, well. See. I don't usually go around kissing dead girls in coffins. That's a bit odd. Also I'm fairly sure it's against the law. Besides, I'm married." He smiled lovingly up at Cinderella. She blew him a kiss.

"But she isn't dead," one of the children said.

"She isn't breathing," Prince Charring said.

"Oh, she never breathes!"

"Have you checked her pulse?" the prince asked.

The children shook their heads. They were only kids. They didn't understand anything about CPR. The prince pushed the lid off the glass coffin, lifting up Snow White's wrist. "I don't feel anything."

"Try her neck!" Cinderella offered helpfully.

The prince couldn't quite reach, so he gently lifted Snow White's head. The piece of blood orange popped right out of her mouth. Her eyes fluttered open. Luckily for him, Prince Charring was looking at her neck, not her eyes.

The hirsute children shoved him out of the way. "Snow White!" they shouted. "Snow White! You're alive!"

"Not exactly," she said. She jumped out of the coffin, grabbing the first child and draining him of what little remained of his blood. He dropped to the ground.

"Oh no!" the prince said. But even as he watched, the child's eyes went from glassy and dead to glowing and red. "Oh, no?" Prince Charring backed up as, one by

176

one, the seven hirsute children were drained. They turned toward him, hissing and baring their sharp teeth. One ran forward, but he tripped on his long beard.

Cinderella grabbed Prince Charring's hand and pulled him up onto the horse. Behind them were seven hirsute children and one beautiful, sweet, good girl chasing them.

And they all lived happily ever after!

Wait, no, sorry, wrong ending. Somehow I don't think this one has a happy ending. Let's jump to the next, instead!

Meanwhile, in one of the few remaining villages . . .

Mary had a little lamb
Little lamb
Little lamb
Mary had a little lamb
Its fleece was white as snow

Everywhere that Mary went
Mary went
Mary went
Everywhere that Mary went
The lamb was sure to go

It followed her to school one day
School one day
School one day

It followed her to school one day
Which was against the rule

It made the authorities come and say
Come and say
Come and say
It made the authorities come and say
You can't do that at school

They took her little lamb away
Lamb away
Lamb away
They took her little lamb away
And made a yummy stew

JUST KIDDING, THAT'S TERRIBLE
They led her little flock away
Flock away
Flock away
They led her little flock away
And gave it to someone new.

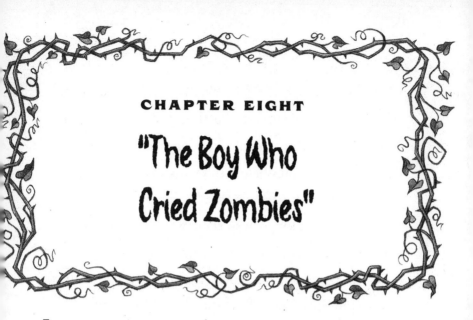

CHAPTER EIGHT

"The Boy Who Cried Zombies"

Jack knew even less about sheep than he did about peas.

Well, that's not quite true. He knew that you should never put sheep up your nose, at least.

After he finally got down from the beanstalk, he had stumbled into a village. The police were taking away a sobbing girl named Mary. "Hey, you!" a police officer had asked. "You go to school?"

"No?" Jack had answered. He attached a question mark because he didn't know if "no" was the answer that got him arrested. Luckily for him, it was not.

"Good. You've got a new job." The police officer had pointed at a flock of sheep on a hill. "You're in charge. Whatever you do, don't take those sheep to school!"

So now Jack had a job! Finally, a chance to redeem himself. He could totally do this. It couldn't be much harder than taking care of a cow, and he did that for like forty whole minutes before screwing everything up.

But this was different. Better. He didn't even go to school, so not taking sheep there was a piece of cake!

The sheep milled about, eating and drinking and doing other various sheepish things. Jack was excited. His stepmother would be so proud to hear he was a successful sheep . . . boy. Sheep person. Sheep-watcher? Sheep-sitter. He really should have asked for more details.

But no matter. He had a job! And he was great at it! All that sitting, watching, not taking the sheep to school. It was just great, super great, really . . .

He didn't like looking at sheep, he realized. Their fluffy white wool reminded him too much of clouds. Horrible, bouncy, giant-filled clouds.

He didn't like talking to the sheep, either. Sheep are terrible conversationalists. He asked how they liked being sheep. "Meh," they answered. He asked if they liked eating grass. "Meh," they answered. He asked if they liked him. That time, they didn't even say anything. They just stared, slowly chewing their meh grass. Jerks.

He stared forlornly down at the village, wishing someone would come visit him. It almost made him miss Jill and her stupid red cloak with its stupid red hood. He wondered what Jill was up to. He wondered what his stepmother was up to. He wondered what beautiful, sweet, good Snow White was up to. He missed her.

Jack flopped down onto his back, groaning in agony. He was so bored and so lonely! (I should note that, at this point, he had been watching the sheep for approximately seventeen minutes.) If only someone would come visit him.

He stood, looking down at the tiny figures in the village below. "Knock, knock!" he shouted.

No one answered.

"Who's there?" Jack muttered to himself. "Ewe!" he said. "Ewe who? Well, yoo-hoo to you, too!"

"Meh," a sheep said.

Jack threw a handful of grass at the sheep. "That was a great joke! I hope you get eaten by wolves!" he shouted.

"Wolves?" someone down at the village cried out. "Wolves? Wolves!"

Suddenly, the whole village was surging out of their homes, running up the hill toward him. He stood, thrilled. Finally some visitors! They arrived out of breath, holding knives, pitchforks, and one flamethrower. (That is not actually how you want visitors to show up. Unless you have a very different sort of party than I normally do.)

"Where is the wolf?" a burly man with a burly mustache asked.

"Yes, where?" a thin man with a thin mustache asked.

"Wolves?" Jack asked. "Who said anything about wolves?"

"You did!" a curvy woman with a curvy mustache shouted. (She, too, was hirsute. She won all the mustache contests. Everyone was jealous.)

"I was just trying to tell a knock-knock joke!"

The curvy woman smacked him in the side of the head. "Well, knock knock it off! I have pies in the oven." Grumbling, she tromped back down the hill, followed by the rest of the villagers and possibly one of the sheep. I wasn't paying attention. Neither was their sheep-sitter.

Jack rubbed the side of his head. It hurt from where that horrible woman with the wonderful mustache had hit him. Now he was bored AND his head hurt. He watched as she went back to the closest house at the bottom of the hill. Jack waited a few minutes, until he was sure her pies would be almost done. Then he stood and, cupping his hands around his mouth, shouted, "WOLVES!"

Again, people swarmed out of their houses and raced up the hill. The mustachioed woman was wearing oven mitts and clutching a hatchet. "Where are the wolves?" she demanded.

Jack looked from side to side, faking innocence. "I could have sworn I saw one. Over there." He pointed into the trees. She ran in, followed by several men. Jack sprinted down the hill to her house. On the table was a glorious apple pie. Jack didn't know about vegetables, but when it came to fruit in pies, he was an expert. Though the pie was so hot it scalded his tongue, he shoved handfuls of it into his mouth.

Then he turned and ran back up the hill.

The villagers came out of the trees. Everyone was frowning. "There was no wolf. No footprints. Are you sure that's what you saw?" the woman demanded.

"Oh, mmmmfff, mmhmm," Jack mumbled, nodding. His mouth was still full of pie. But his belly wasn't full yet. The villagers grumbled, walking slowly back down the hill. When the woman got to her door, Jack managed to swallow the rest of his mouthful.

"Wolf!" he screamed, pointing at the trees. They all ran back—much, much slower this time, because it was a lot of running up and down hills. (In fact, the woman who would go on to invent the tower-stair exercise method would also have a popular "Oh No, Wolf!" hill sprinting class. But she hired actual wolves to chase people up and down the hills for extra motivation. If you survived, you ended up in great shape!)

As soon as they were out of sight, Jack rolled down the hill and back to his pie. He ate the rest of it, and was still licking the crumbs off his fingers as he strolled back to his spot.

"No sign of any wolves," the woman said. But then she stopped, her glorious mustache quivering in anger. She leaned close to Jack—closer—closer. His tongue darted out to lick a stray crumb. She reached out fast as lightning and grabbed his tongue. "Ah ha!" she shouted.

"Whuu ah oo ooing?" Jack said, because it is very hard to talk when someone is holding on to your tongue.

"Apple pie!" she shouted. "There was no wolf! Only a greedy little liar."

"Arrest him!" someone screamed.

"Can't," the mustachioed woman said. "The police are still interrogating Mary. And if we have him arrested, there won't be anyone to watch the sheep." She was still holding on to Jack's tongue, which was getting very uncomfortable. She tugged him forward, pinching his tongue. Then she let him go. "Come on," she grumbled.

Jack watched as everyone went back down the hill. They were setting up lights in the village square. It looked like some sort of party. Jack had no doubt he was no longer invited, if he ever had been.

The sun set. He was cold. He had eaten too much pie, and now he was thirsty. And his tongue hurt from being burned and then tugged on.

"I deserve better than this," Jack whined.

"Meh," said the sheep.

A twig snapped in the trees behind him. Jack startled, peering deep into the darkness there. A flash of red eyes peered back at him, then disappeared.

"Wolf," he whispered.

Another twig snapped. Jack whipped his head to the side, where a second set of red eyes watched him.

"Wolf," he said.

A chorus of low growls sounded.

"Wolves!" Jack shouted. "Wolves, wolves, wolves!" He looked down the hill, waiting for the villagers to run up with their wonderful knives and clubs and flamethrowers. But no one was coming.

Then the wolves began to howl. Jack had always hated the sound of wolves howling. It was so lonely, so forlorn, and so menacing all at the same time. But this time, it sounded . . . different.

"Braaaaaaiiiiiins!" the wolves howled.

"Meh?" a sheep asked.

Jack stumbled backward, afraid to take his eyes off the trees.

"Wolves!" he shouted until his voice was hoarse. "Wolves, wolves, wolves!!!"

Slowly, five wolves shambled from under the pitch black cover of the trees. Their eyes glowed. Their bodies were hunched and twisted. They had none of the sleek grace of predators. Instead, they lurched brokenly, mouths hanging open.

"Brains," they growled.

"Zombies?" Jack whimpered. But he knew it didn't

matter. No one was coming to help him. He had cried wolf too many times. He certainly couldn't cry "zombie" and expect a different result. Now he was going to die, and the whole village would, too, all because he had been bored. (There are much better things to do when you are bored. You can read a book, or write a story. Start a glass coffin collection. Go spin in circles until you throw up. Clean the house. [Your parents paid me to put that one in here, sorry.] Basically do anything other than be the reason an entire village is about to be eaten by zombie wolves. That's a terrible thing to do just because you are bored.)

The lead wolf staggered toward him. Jack clutched the nearest sheep. At least he wouldn't die alone. The sheep kicked Jack in the stomach. "You're on your own, kid," it said, before running off with the other sheep.

"Oh, so *now* you can talk?" Jack cried after it. He looked into the horrible eyes of his doom. "Meh," he whimpered.

And then, out of nowhere, a gleaming golden lock flew into the wolf's head. "Get up!" someone shouted, tugging on Jack's arm.

Jack scrambled to his feet. A little girl with beautiful golden locks of hair stood between him and death. She swung another thick lock around and around on a golden chain. A zombie wolf came at them from the side, and, before Jack could cry out, the girl had flung the lock at its head, knocking it down. She pulled the lock back, wrapping the chain around her wrist.

"There are more coming," she said grimly. (Many fairy tales are grim. A lot of them are Grimm, too.) "We have to go warn the village."

Jack had no sheep, but he was very sheepish. "You might want to be the one to tell them. I don't

think they'll believe me. I broke into a house and ate all the food."

Goldilocks shrugged. "I don't see the problem with that, as long as it was just right." She sprinted down the hill.

Jack risked one look back. He really shouldn't have. An army of zombie woodland creatures, along with most of the castle employees and one burly woodcutter, were coming out of the trees. A girl in a red riding hood lurched to the front.

"Jill?" he asked.

She turned toward him, her eyes glowing. "Braaaaaiiiiins," she growled.

Jack fell down the hill.

Jill came tumbling after.

Meanwhile, Jack . . .

Jack be nimble, Jack be quick,
Jack jump over the candlestick!

Jack be wary, Jack be brave,
Jack jump over the open grave!

Jack be speedy, Jack be fast,
Jack jump out of that zombie's grasp!

Jack be clever, Jack be strong,
Jack jump deathtraps the whole night long!

Jack be weary, Jack beware,
Jack, jump back to Stepmother's care!

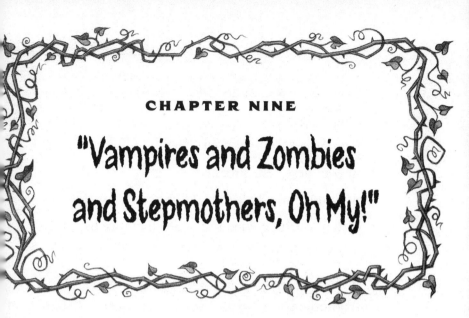

CHAPTER NINE

"Vampires and Zombies and Stepmothers, Oh My!"

Once upon a time, there was a stepmother who had devoted her life to putting out fires.

Whether they were metaphorical fires, like a stepdaughter destined to grow into a terrible creature of the night or a stepdaughter who fell victim to her horrible hungry pet, or literal fires, like the kind she had been dumping water on all day thanks to Cinderella and Prince Charring's honeymoon tour through the kingdom, the stepmother was there to put them out.

She had just finished dousing a literal fire, and was not ready to douse any metaphorical fires. So when she heard Jack screaming her name, she sat heavily onto the ground and put her head in her hands. A little dog trotted by. Its bark sounded like it was laughing to see such a sight.

"Stepmother!" Jack shouted. "Stepmoooooooother!"

"I'm over here," she groaned.

Jack skidded to a halt in front of her. At his side was a girl with beautiful golden locks. She had nice hair, too. "We need your help!"

"Of course you do."

"Stepmother!" a girl's voice screamed. "Stepmoooooooooother!"

The stepmother stood, puzzled. From the opposite direction, a horse came barreling out of the trees. Cinderella and Prince Charring clung to its back. They didn't even have anything burning with them. Something must really be wrong.

"We need your help!" the prince shouted.

"No, we need her help!" Jack said. He pointed in the direction he had come from. "Zombies!"

Cinderella scowled, pointing back to the trees where she had come from. "Vampires!"

The stepmother massaged her temples. She had a headache. She had had a headache for approximately the last eighteen years. "Zombies?"

"Yes," the girl with the golden locks said. "I've been tracking the source of the outbreak for days. Fortunately, they bypassed the sheep village. Their leader seems to be especially hungry for Jack's brains. She's a little girl in a red riding hood."

"Jill?" The stepmother looked at Jack. Jack shrugged sheepishly, the one skill he had learned while being a sheep-sitter.

"There are too many for me to fight on my own." Goldilocks twirled one of her weapons, watching the night for signs of shambling.

"Well, we have vampires!" Cinderella said. "A creepy girl and seven little dwarves!"

"Hirsute boys," the stepmother corrected.

"Hirsute vampires," Prince Charring updated.

It was the middle of the night. There was no sun. And even if there was sun, the stepmother didn't know how to deal with zombies. She thought she had taken care of Snow White—twice!—but something always came up. It was all Jack and Cinderella's fault. If they hadn't been climbing plants up into the clouds or setting fires, she would have been able to make sure that Snow White had been properly and permanently put to sleep. And where had the zombies come from?

(Should I tell her? No, she's better off not knowing. I wish I didn't know.)

"I don't think I care," the stepmother said.

"What?" Jack asked.

"I'm tired. I've been cleaning up messes for eighteen years now, ever since I took my first job as a stepmother. What's wrong with these kingdoms, anyway? Why are there no mothers? Why do all the fathers up and die as soon as they marry me? It's not fair! It's not fair, and I'm not going to do it anymore. All this time I thought I was helping you all. Now I think maybe I was hurting."

"But we need you!" Cinderella said.

The stepmother took off wedding ring after wedding ring, dropping them onto the ground. "What you need," she said as the last ring plinked metallically to the pile, "is to figure out how to deal with your own problems."

"Umm, this is a little more serious than help with homework," Goldilocks said.

"It's all the same principle. You have brains. You have skills." She paused, frowning at Jack. "Well, you have *something*. Use it."

"But what are you going to do?" Jack asked.

The stepmother pulled out all she had left in her bag. A dish and a spoon. Maybe she could use them to—

The dish grabbed the spoon and ran away. Even dishes have enough sense to leave when caught between a vampire army and a zombie horde.

"Well, I'm going to go sleep." Dusting off her skirts, the stepmother climbed the nearest tree. She had barely settled onto a nice, comfortable branch when she heard cooing. She peered over to see a cradle, complete with baby.

"Oh, great. I don't suppose you have a mother, do you?"

The baby clapped its hands and giggled.

"Do you like fire?"

The baby shook its head.

"Are you secretly undead?"

The baby laughed, blowing bubbles.

"Honestly, this kingdom." The stepmother patted the baby's stomach until it fell asleep. Then, closing her eyes, she did, too.

Down on the ground, Cinderella, Prince Charring, Goldilocks, and Jack stared at each other. "Goldilocks can fight," Jack said.

"Not that many zombies at once. And I've never fought vampires."

Cinderella looked at her hands helplessly. They were filled with matches. "What do the rest of us have to offer?"

"I had a cow," Jack said sadly.

"What good would a cow do us?" Goldilocks asked.

"We'll never know, because I traded her for some magic beans."

Prince Charring snapped his fingers. "Magic beans! Yes! We'll use those!"

Jack shook his head. "I don't have them anymore. I accidentally planted them and they grew into a huge stalk."

"Oh." Cinderella pulled out a lighter, flicking it on and off, on and off. It wasn't comforting her much right now. "Well, what do we know about zombies and vampires?"

"They don't like sunlight," Goldilocks said. "But we've got too many hours left in the night."

"Hmm." The prince rubbed two sticks together, lighting a small pile of hay on fire. "If only there was something else that both vampires and zombies feared. Something we could use. Something we were good at."

200

Jack nodded, morose. *Morose* is like *sad*, when you have even *more* sad, but you have to keep going regardless.

"It wouldn't matter anyway," Jack said. "The whole kingdom is blocked in by giant plants. So they're trapped in here, and we are, too."

Goldilocks paced. "If only there was somewhere else we could send them, and some way to scare them into going there!"

Jack sat on the ground, defeated. "I guess we're all going to be eaten."

THE END

"Wait," Jack said, staring up at those letters. "I don't want this to be the end! Stepmother is right. I'm thinking short-term again. I need to think long-term. She said we already had everything we needed!"

Goldilocks patted his shoulder sympathetically. "Yes, then she climbed up a tree and went to sleep. Maybe her advice isn't super dependable."

"What are you good at?" Jack asked Cinderella and Prince Charring.

They both held up torches in response.

"And what are you good at?" Jack asked Goldilocks.

"Breaking and entering, mostly. But I used to herd sheep. They called me Little Bo Peep."

"My snake is good at eating things." They all turned in surprise to see a tall, round girl with a long, thick snake. The prince yelped in terror, jumping into Cinderella's arms.

"How *many* things?" Jack asked hopefully. "We have, like, a few dozen . . . things . . . that need to be eaten!"

"Not that many," Rapunzel said. "Even my fair Herr has his limits."

Jack didn't have time to ask for a spelling clarification. "Darn. So your snake can eat a few things.

Goldilocks is good at herding things. And they're good at fire." Jack frowned. He rubbed his forehead. If only he still had his magic beans! If only he had a way for them to get those zombies and vampires out of the kingdom! If only—

"Fee fie foe fum," Jack muttered. His brown eyes grew wide. "I have an idea?" he asked. (He asked because he had never really had an idea before, and he wasn't sure what they felt like. But I know. Yes, Jack! You're having an idea!) "If zombies and vampires don't like the sun, they definitely won't like fire. The sun is made out of fire, after all. And we can use fire and Goldilock's herding skills to get them where we want them. And the snake can eat any stragglers!"

"Where do we want them?" Prince Charring asked.

Jack pointed to the sky. Against the dark of the night, a single black stalk could be seen. "The only way out of the kingdom is up. We drive them to the beanstalk, they climb, and then we chop it down when they're all gone!"

Goldilocks threw her arms around Jack's neck. "That's perfect!"

"We need more supplies," Cinderella said. "Gasoline, wood, gasoline, cloth, gasoline, matches, gasoline . . ."

"Books," Prince Charring suggested. *No!* I shout. *You cannot have any books!* Prince Charring rubbed his ears. "Fine, fine, no books."

Rapunzel stroked her fair Herr and gave him a pep talk. The prince stayed very far away from both of them.

Goldilocks ran from house to house, breaking and entering. Normally, I would chide her for violating the law, but tonight I'll cheer her on. Go, Goldilocks, go! Find those houses that are just right!

Cinderella and Prince Charring followed, gathering everything flammable and inflammable (which inexplicably mean the same thing, because no one asked me if that made any sense before they decided that) they could find. Except books, because Prince Charring didn't want to make me angry. They already had to deal with angry zombies and angry vampires, after all. And nothing is more terrifying than angry narrators.

Once everything was in place, all that was left to do was wait.

Jack hated waiting. He always got bored. But he had finally found a good solution to boredom: sheer and utter terror! He was so scared, he couldn't even manage to complain about having to stand alone in the middle of the road.

Fortunately, he didn't have to wait there long. Led by Red Riding Hood, the zombie horde shambled and lurched toward him. On the other end of the road, Snow White emerged from the night. Her smile was sharper than a knife. Behind her were the seven hirsute vampires. When Snow White saw Jack, she hissed. Jack had been the queen's favorite. Spoiled. Free. Snow White wanted his blood more than anyone else's! But she'd have to compete with Red Riding Hood, who wanted his *brains* more than anyone else's.

Jack trembled. All *he* wanted—all he ever wanted—was something good to eat and a comfy place for a nap. But he had finally learned that you have to earn those things. "Oh boy!" he shouted. "I sure do have a large, juicy brain! And so much blood you can practically hear me sloshing when I run!"

All the red zombie eyes and all the glowing vampire eyes turned and fixed on Jack. Jack, be nimble! Jack, BE QUICK! Jack darted into the forest. Behind him, he heard hissing and growling, shambling and darting, groans for his brains and sweet cheerful calls for some of his blood, please.

He nearly turned around. Snow White was so beautiful, and so good, and so sweet! But he knew Jill was back there, too, with her little red riding hood. And she was not good or sweet! So he kept running.

Jack was getting tired, but he pushed himself even faster. Most of this was his fault, after all. When this was over, he was going to learn the name of every single vegetable in the world. He might even eat some of them! Finally he saw the beanstalk up ahead of him.

He ran past it and skidded to a halt on the far side. The vampires and zombies were almost to him. "Now!" he shouted. Cinderella and Prince Charring put their torches to the ground, and an impassable ring of fire *fwooshed* up in a circle around the base of the beanstalk. Snow White screamed and cried, batting her eyelashes and crying pitiful tears. Little Red Riding Hood stood so close to the flames Jack could smell her cooking. It cured his appetite.

Goldilocks ran around the perimeter, making sure no creatures escaped their trap. The fair Herr ate one wolf, one burly woodsman, and a single hirsute vampire. It was hard to slither anymore with three such large lumps inside, but Rapunzel clapped her hands in glee. "Who's a good fair Herr? You are! Yes, you are!"

"That's everyone!" Goldilocks shouted. "No more stragglers!"

"Just go!" Jack shouted at Jill. She was still trying to get through the fire to him. "It's too hot!"

Even in her current state, Little Red Riding Hood knew that, for once, this *too* was too much. Following her lead, the vampires and zombies started climbing the beanstalk.

Up,

up,

up they climbed.

When the last trailing groan of "braaaaaaiiiiiins" had faded away to nothing, and Jack couldn't hear Snow White's tempting song anymore, Goldilocks handed Jack an ax.

She grinned. "You do the honors."

Jack swung the ax with all his might. It hit the base

of the beanstalk, and . . . barely made a dent. You really do need to start eating your vegetables, Jack. Panting for breath, he took another swing, then another. Rapunzel, impatient, took the ax from him. She had enormous muscles from hauling such a heavy snake up and down her tower. After three powerful swings, the beanstalk fell with a mighty crash. It knocked down trees and homes, even taking out part of the vine wall around the kingdom.

Jack stood proudly with his hands on his hips. As the sun rose over the smoldering, burning, smoking, broken, smashed, depopulated ruins of the kingdom, Jack and the gang patted one another on the back. "We saved everyone!" they cheered.

They slowly picked their way through the fires to where they had left the stepmother. She was standing beneath her tree, holding a baby.

"Rapunzel!" she said, using her free arm to hug the black-clad, Mohawked girl. "I thought you'd been eaten!"

"My fair Herr would never!"

If the snake could talk, he would have said, "Never

say never. But not today." His tummy hurt from all that undead dinner.

"Who is that?" Jack asked, pointing to the baby.

"I think I'll name her Little Miss Muffet."

Jack was very glad his stepmother had adopted him *after* he had already been named. But he grinned. "You were right. We did it! We used what we already had. We didn't even need you." Jack recounted the tale, complete with sound effects and a few fire flourishes from Cinderella and Prince Charring. "And then, when they were all up there, we chopped down the beanstalk!"

Rapunzel cleared her throat, flexing her muscles menacingly.

"Well, *Rapunzel* chopped down the beanstalk, technically. But we all worked together."

The stepmother nodded approvingly. "I can't believe it, but you did it. And you even managed to save Jill and Snow White." She wiped a tear from her eye. "You gave them a new home, where they can be free! And where there's no one for them to turn into more vampires or zombies."

Jack smiled even bigger. And then he stopped smiling. "Oh, well. Umm. The cloud land isn't *exactly* empty."

Oh no.

Oh, *no*.

FEE

FIE

FOE

FUM,

JACK,

THAT

PLAN

WAS

REALLY

DUMB...

THE END

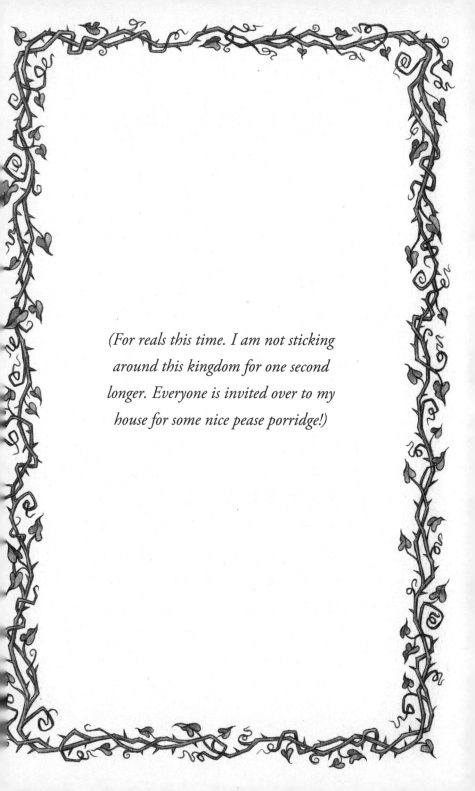

(For reals this time. I am not sticking around this kingdom for one second longer. Everyone is invited over to my house for some nice pease porridge!)

Acknowledgments

Once upon a time, an editor emailed me and said, "You know those fairy tale jokes you made on Twitter? I think there's a book idea there, and I want it." The editor was bright of mind and lively of heart, the Black to my White, and very right. There *was* a book idea there, and, thanks to Erin Black's encouragement and insight, you just read it. I hope. It's weird if you're reading the acknowledgments first. Maybe you meant to cheat and read the end of the book and accidentally read this instead, in which case, SHAME ON YOU, GO BACK AND START AT THE BEGINNING.

So, thank you, Erin Black, for being a girl with a secret monster heart and loving literary strolls in silly dark woods. Thank you to everyone at Scholastic for joining us for a picnic with a wolf or two. Thank you to Carol Ly for the frighteningly perfect page design. Thank you to Karl Kwasny for such disturbingly delightful art. You're all worth more than a handful of magic beans. And way, way more than a handful of peas.

Thank you to my agent, Michelle Wolfson, who thought it all sounded too scary but was willing to work with it anyway. I'm always so much scarier than you think I'll be. We short girls are sneaky like that.

Thank you to my very own prince (who always practices the strictest levels of fire safety), Noah, and to our three delightful and well-behaved children, Elena, Jonah, and Ezra. They helped with my vocabulary, and can spell well enough to save all our lives should the need arise. Kids, if you promise never to get pet snakes, I promise never to make pease porridge.

Finally, thank YOU. Yes, you! No, not *you*. Just kidding, even you! Thank you for reading. I've been trying to write the right book for kids just like you my whole career. I'm so happy it's in your hands now. I hope you loved it! And if you didn't, please bring all complaints to my friend, the fair Herr. He's dying to eat you. I mean, meet you. Yes. Meet you.

About the Author

KIERSTEN WHITE is the acclaimed bestselling author of *And I Darken*, the Paranormalcy trilogy, the Mind Games series, *The Chaos of Stars*, *Illusions of Fate*, and *In the Shadows* (with artist Jim Di Bartolo). She lives in San Diego with her husband and three children. Her life is as happy as a stroll through a dark wood with a full picnic basket. Visit her online at www.kierstenwhite.com.